★ ★ ★ ★ ★

"I'd like to introduce you to the mistress of tactical military fiction. You will appreciate how Adair paints a true portrait of the Special Operations world without drowning you in technobabble. Like the operators she writes about, Adair is up front and to the point. *Shadow Game* is a swift read and reminds us all what a 'thriller' is supposed to be. Adair's writing is a refreshing glass of water in a desert of comic book hero fantasy."

—Zakhdit

"Attention all spy novel enthusiasts: This is your new series! Baldacci meets Clancy in this riveting modern-day spy versus evil adventure. Great read—highly recommend!"

—Alan

"I didn't know how much I needed thriller books in my life until I met Elle Anderson and her spec ops team. If you're new to the thriller genre as a female, this is a great book to start with because Elle is an empowering character from beginning to end. *Shadow Game* is a smooth read and the story is constantly evolving. I could not put it down."

—Taylor Hufford

"A. M. Adair is an awesome first-time novelist. The author's creativity draws you into the story and lives of the characters."

—Luther G. Yoda

"Masterful. This novel allows readers to immerse themselves in the dark, murky, shadowy world of clandestine operations. It not only illustrates the adrenaline highs of a surreptitious operation but also captures the deep emotional and psychological tolls the lifestyle has for everyone involved. Brilliant work."

—Anonymous

"A. M. Adair hit this one out of the park! Elle Anderson is a badass female version of Vince Flynn's CIA anti-terrorism assassin Mitch Rapp. I couldn't put this one down, and I can't wait to continue this thriller series when The Deeper Shadow comes out."

—Daniel Farish

"The author knows the unique heart of courage, mental brilliance, and fierceness that women in the field require! Adair has made female military leaders and career professionals proud!"

—Anjenelle Kelly

"This book had me hooked from the start. I'm an avid reader of the Mitch Rapp American Assassin series and Jack Ryan. Elle Anderson fits right in with those two as a badass, easy-to-root-for protagonist. Highly recommend if you enjoy espionage thrillers. Ready for Book 2!"

—Joshua Brautigam

"A refreshing twist that wasn't just a modern wild west story running and gunning remake. It's great seeing a strong female role that feels as genuine and believable as Elle."

—Bjorn

THE
DEEPER
SHADOW

AN ELLE ANDERSON NOVEL

Dave,
Hope you're
enjoying the series!

A. M. ADAIR

STORY MERCHANT BOOKS
LOS ANGELES • 2020

The Deeper Shadow

ISBN-13: 978-1-970157-25-3

Story Merchant Books
400 S. Burnside Avenue, #11B
Los Angeles, CA 90036
www.storymerchantbooks.com

www.529bookdesign.com
Interior: Lauren Michelle

www.designartstudio.net
Cover: Hargun Singh

Author Facebook: A. M. Adair

THE
DEEPER
SHADOW

A. M. ADAIR

For Mom and Dad

THE DEEPER SHADOW

PROLOGUE

I *should have let her die.* CIA Director Markus Calloway stood frozen at the window of his office in Langley. He had allowed a covert operation to deviate from protocol. Black Ops agents were supposed to be on their own if captured or compromised, but he had supported a rescue mission. There would be repercussions. How bad would the fallout be? Did the CIA still have deniability?

The silence was shattered by ringing on his private line. Glancing at the caller ID, he answered without preamble, "What's her status?"

"She's unconscious, and her status is guarded. They've stopped the bleeding and removed several blood clots that would have killed her. She'll probably need more surgeries in the coming days," Agent Mike Traviano said with an uneasy strain in his voice.

"Your partner has a fighting chance because of you, Mr. Traviano."

"Thank you, sir. We'll keep the pressure on the network until Elle returns."

"Ms. Anderson will be out of commission for some time, and we need to follow the proper procedures.

Your team needs to come in for debriefing, and then you'll step in for her and eliminate the target list."

"All due respect, sir, but proper procedures won't get results in this scenario. Elle proved that. I would like to propose we pull together a new list that will keep the network in chaos and buy time for Elle to recover. I can integrate with the SOF unit here, leverage those resources, and build some positive PR for the Agency. When I hit a point where we need to be more surgical, I'll pull in the shooters that have already worked with us to limit further exposure."

"You've been working with Ms. Anderson long enough that you should be able to pick up where she left off. It's the smart play and the most logical course of action. Why aren't you advocating for that?"

"Because I owe Elle my life."

"I would say you've repaid that debt, Agent."

"No, sir. I'm not talking about three years ago. I'm talking about now. If she hadn't insisted on coming with me on that op, it would have been me captured and tortured. We're responsible for what happened."

"Ms. Anderson knew the risks, and she accepted them."

"Elle would say the same thing. And she's going to be pissed when she realizes that I came for her after she ordered me not to."

"Ms. Anderson is a unique individual in many ways, but she's still human. I have serious doubts she'll ever be physically or mentally able to continue as a field operative, let alone a team leader, after what she went through."

"Please, sir, just give us a chance to see this through. We owe her that much. She gets results. We can kill these guys at any time, but more names will just keep popping up in their place. If Elle succeeds, the network won't be able to recover, they'll be crippled permanently."

The seconds dragged on like days as Calloway weighed his options.

CHAPTER 1

Three Months Later

A scream lodged in her throat, choking her awake. Elle Anderson looked around wildly. It took a while to recognize the place. She was back in the United States at Walter Reed Medical Center. Since her transfer here a month back, she'd been having these episodes. "Night terrors," one doctor said. She was on medication to help with sleep, but it didn't always work. It was like the dreams would build up and crush her every time she closed her eyes.

She denied having issues, but she screamed in that dream state, cried, begged for help, threatened vengeance. She fought her captors over and over. One night, the third shift tried to restrain her so she wouldn't hurt herself. It was disastrous. A few bloody lips and a broken nose ended that tactic. They couldn't tie her down. Not after what the terrorists had done to her.

Her damp hospital gown clung to her skin, and she stank of sweat. She rubbed her neck, noting that her skin and hairline were still wet. This confirmed the night terrors and made her chest tighten painfully. It was hard to convince the elite Walter Reed medical team she was fine during the day when her mind and body disobeyed and betrayed her every night. In many ways, she was still back in Iraq, vulnerable and tied to that chair.

She would push past this and be fine. She didn't need to be coddled.

Elle glanced at the clock on the wall and saw that it was just past two in the morning. She got out of bed and paced the room. Her heart thundered in her chest. She needed to move. This was shaping up to be her new ritual. Elle had always been a light sleeper and rarely stayed in bed long. Still, she never had any issues with sleep before, unless disturbed. No matter how exhausted she was from another day of physical therapy, it was a battle to sleep at night.

Maybe the lack of sleep was what was keeping her from being able to regain control?

Forcing herself to lie back in bed, she puzzled over that possibility as her heart rate slowed, and her body started to feel heavy. She shifted her weight and felt a sharp pain in response. Her mind might not be functioning as it should, but she was hitting her physical therapy program at full force. Consequently, her body felt battered, and she was constantly in pain. Elle threw herself into the program with an almost manic determination. Her therapists and doctors had counseled caution, but she brushed off their concerns. She was determined to push hard and get back to full strength. There was no other option.

Her eyes found the call button, and she debated about asking for painkillers. *No. Get off the damn drugs.* While she'd been in worse pain before, this was different. Her mind betrayed her nightly, her body during the day. There was never any respite from the torture.

Lying in her hospital bed, Elle thought about how far she had let herself fall, which brought on a feeling of bleakness. Then, without warning, she was crying. Denial couldn't stop the flow of tears. She felt wildly out of control. Elle had considered her emotions a nuisance before the capture—that didn't even compare to what was happening now. More often than not, she was angry. It would be instant, fiery, and without any rational basis.

Alone, no one would question her tears, and she wouldn't have to see the pity on peoples' faces. So, she let the tears flow, not fighting it this time.

Elle had no idea what was wrong, but the severity of her wounds had triggered concerns of brain damage from oxygen deprivation due to an insufficient blood supply. Blood clots had developed and had nearly killed her. Ironically, those same clots had caused a temporary lack-of-pain response, which had allowed her to function beyond normal limits and escape her captors. They saved her life. The doctors all agreed she had been lucky to survive, but she had recognized the different cognitive tests for what they were.

It should never have happened.

Elle and her team had been sent in by the CIA to destroy Daesh, known to the world as ISIS. From the start, things had not gone as planned. Interference from higher up had forced her hand, and the results had been catastrophic. Her capture had been orchestrated by one of her targets—a Syrian cleric named Mahmud Hussein, number 3 on her hit list. He had provided information to the U.S. Government to have his rivals taken out. His plan worked. And, as a bonus, he had set a trap by providing more information that ensured Elle's superiors would send her directly into his clutches. His intention was to torture and use her for propaganda before killing her. She barely survived the attempt but succeeded in wounding Hussein during her escape.

Hussein could tie her to one assassination, but she had gotten away clean. Now, he'd never be able to convince anyone of her guilt without exposing his own. There was some comfort in knowing that five of her targets were already dead, but that meant six more were still out there. The mission wasn't over. Most nights, she found herself running through her target list over and over.

2, 3, 4, 6, 7, 9….

2, 3, 4, 6, 7, 9. No names. Just target numbers.

As the room started to lighten from the approaching dawn, Elle fell back asleep, only to be startled awake a short time later by a nurse bringing in breakfast. Elle reflexively masked her alarm at the sudden intrusion— a new habit of hers. She knew how to put on a façade and counted on that skill to help her get past the staff. Her heart was still pounding, but she smiled and thanked the orderly. Years of experience reading people and situations was, once again, proving invaluable. But, unfortunately, the few key people she needed on her side were proving difficult to sway.

Elle ate and got ready for the day's events. Looking at the board with the day's schedule confirmed that she had yet another evaluation on the docket. She felt better equipped to handle this one and was confident they would see she was ready to be discharged.

As she was preparing to leave her room, breaking news flashed across the TV screen. Muhammad Kalash was dead. Number 4 on her target list had been taken out in a joint operation between U.S. Special Operations and the Iraqi Army. *Please let this be a coincidence.* Behind every news report about a terrorist being killed, there was someone working from the shadows who made it happen. That someone was usually her. Elle grabbed the bedside telephone and dialed her boss directly.

"It's only been a week since you last called, Ms. Anderson. My answer hasn't changed. Your status is under review, and you need to be evaluated, so we have nothing further to discuss at this time," Director Calloway said.

"That's not why—Muhammad Kalash was killed during a joint op, sir. Yes?" Elle couldn't go into detail on an open line, but she didn't have to.

"Progress is key, Ms. Anderson."

Elle felt liked she'd been kicked. Her head was spinning. Her team had been ordered to continue on without her. They had been trying to keep Daesh in chaos long enough to give her time to return to finish dismantling them. She'd taken too long. And now they moved on and had made a big mistake. "Sir, you need to bring me back in. We can't finish things this way. It will bring them back together, and the network will go on the attack. Lives will be lost."

"I understand your concern and attachment to this, but you need to let it go. You may be surprised to learn that we existed before you came along, and we can continue without you. We have many talented people working on this problem set, and we will see it through one way or the other. Now, you need to focus on what's in front of you. I will continue to monitor your progress. Once you are cleared, we can schedule a time to discuss what's next."

"Sir, please—"

"We're done here, Ms. Anderson." Calloway hung up.

Rage and a feeling of helplessness consumed her. She ripped the phone out of the wall and threw it at the TV screen. The cheap plastic broke apart, and the screen showed a divot from the impact. The Agency probably wasn't covering that.

The noise made the duty nurse come running into her room.

Elle took several deep breaths. "Sorry. I'll pay for the damage."

"It's time for your assessment, Ms. Anderson," the nurse said.

Elle straightened up as best she could and nodded, avoiding eye contact. Hopefully, this little incident wouldn't hold her back. She gave herself one last look in the mirror, squared her shoulders, and walked out.

No one saw what she did. Elle could care less that 4 was dead; it was the way he died that bothered her. Just killing the targets on her list wouldn't cripple the network: it would strengthen those who remained. The group needed to be destroyed from within; they needed to turn on each other. Elle would have made Daesh believe that one of their own had murdered 4. External threats only tightened their bonds.

CHAPTER 2

Elle knocked on the door of the lead psychiatrist's office.

"Come in."

That was her cue. Elle didn't recognize the man sitting behind the desk reading a file, most likely hers. She stood just inside the door.

"Ms. Elizabeth Anderson, I assume. Please, come in."

Elle winced at the use of her given name. Made her sound like a character in a Jane Austen novel. "Please, call me Elle." Resigned, she sat down in the chair in front of the desk. He was an older gentleman, probably in his late fifties, with a full head of white hair and an easy smile. She was thrown off by the change in doctor, one that didn't look so cookie-cutter. He looked military. Navy?

He regarded her for a moment. "What would you like to have happen here today, Elle?"

She was taken off guard. Weighing her words carefully, she said, "I'm here for my assessment, as directed."

The man gave a half grin. "You can drop the pretense, Elle. I'm not your enemy, and you need help to accept what has happened and to deal with the fallout."

"I don't know who you are or what you think you know about me, but I don't need your help—other than to sign the papers to let me get back to work."

"So, you believe you're special? That you can go through an incredibly traumatic event, nearly die, and have to rebuild all of your physical capability without any emotional or mental scars?"

"You have no idea what I've been through."

"You're right, I don't. You refuse to talk to anyone about it. But I do have access to your medical files. You didn't end up nearly dying on the operating table in Germany playing charades. The severity and abundance of the wounds tell a very gruesome story on their own. And you didn't answer my questions."

Her blood started pounding in her ears. Elle felt trapped again. This time, by a question. Did she think she was special? That sounded so petty and arrogant, but wasn't that really what she thought? It didn't sit right with her, but the alternative was just as bad. "That's not a fair question."

"How so? You want everyone to believe that you are somehow impervious to PTSD. So, you're in denial, special, or have some secret way of coping that we don't have any metric for. If it's the last one, you really should be sharing it so that we can help others."

"Is it so hard to just accept that I'm fine and to let me get on with my life?"

"Is it so hard to just accept that you're not fine and to let us help you?"

Elle really didn't like the direction this was going in. She much preferred the bleeding hearts who just wanted her to cry with them. "Shit happens, it's done. Now, why don't you just stamp my papers and let me leave?"

"As soon as you answer my questions. This can either be a productive conversation, and I can excuse you on schedule, or you can keep being a stubborn jackass and stay here longer. I'm not going to waste your time or mine. You can either work with me, or not— and go back to making everyone, including yourself, miserable. And while I'm sure the second option sounds peachy keen, it's not going to get you cleared to return to work any faster."

He held her gaze. He wasn't bluffing. They sat in silence for a minute, neither breaking eye contact.

At least this guy didn't seem to be bullshitting her. "Fine, what do you want from me?"

"Let's start by agreeing to level with each other. You don't have to like me, but you do have to cooperate. I'm here to make sure that you get the help you need. So, let's begin. Is this conscious denial or are you delusional?"

"Fuck you."

"Lash out all you want, Elle, but it wouldn't bother you so much if there weren't some truth in there."

She leaned back in her chair, crossed her arms across her chest, and regarded her new rival with contempt. Her anger was boiling, but her stomach felt like it had dropped out. She felt the truth of what he was saying, but her mind screamed denials. All she could think about was getting out of this office before she said or did something that would end in more therapy. The man didn't seem phased by her behavior. His calm and collected demeanor just pissed her off more.

"Well, it would seem that we're not going to get anywhere today. We'll postpone your assessment until tomorrow. That way, you can think about what I've asked you and consider this: Accepting what happened does not mean you are weak. Accepting that your life will never be the same does not have to define you. Accepting help will get you back to where you want to be faster and keep you from backsliding. Until you do that, the symptoms of PTSD will get worse, not better."

He walked to the door and opened it, indicating her time was up. Elle fought back several caustic retorts, clenching her jaw so hard her teeth hurt. She got up to storm out of the room but was taken by surprise again. She had barely registered that the man had walked with a pronounced limp and a cane, until now. The way the material of his pants gathered at odd angles around his ankles drew her attention. Combined with his gait and the cane, it could only mean one thing: he was a double amputee, wearing prosthetics on both legs.

Her anger instantly quelled, and she found herself staring at the man, trying to put him into context. He had seen action and paid dearly for it. That type of person didn't fit in with her perception of a so-called mental health professional. Elle found herself confused and unsettled. She didn't bother to hide her dismay and stared openly at him. He just stood there with the same half-grin he'd given her earlier. That look should have made her mad all over again, but her anger didn't reignite.

"Do you still want to leave? Or are you ready to get to work?" he asked.

Elle still didn't want to talk to him. Her throat constricted, and her stomach churned, but she found herself sitting back down.

He settled back into his chair, too. "My name is Dr. Wise, and Calloway asked me to evaluate you. Once upon a time, I was Special Forces. It was all I ever wanted to be and what I worked toward my entire life. It was all that I was. My world revolved around the job.

Then one day, it was taken away from me. It's been fifteen years, and I can still feel the heat of the explosion that hit me a split second before everything went dark. And then the pain when the lights came back on, seeing the carnage all around me. Men who were closer to me than blood, gone. I didn't even realize that my legs were shredded until I tried to get up. Everything changed for me after that. I went to very dark places, and it took a lot to fight my way back. The CIA recruited me to work with field agents because I understand that life. I chose to continue to serve this way since I know better than most what battles are ahead. Now, you can either accept my assistance, and we can move forward, or you can try and go it on your own. I can promise you, if you choose the latter, you will fail no matter how strong you think you are."

What the hell am I supposed to say to that?

Wise sat in silence, watching her calmly.

"Why didn't you tell me who you were from the start?"

"You know why. I would have gotten a performance. This way, we got down to business so much faster," he said.

"What do you want me to say? I'm sorry I was a jackass. If you really understand what the job means to me, then we don't need to go through this. I need to get back to work. It's important."

"If this had happened to one of your team members, would you be pushing them to get back to work?"

"That's different."

"How?

Again, the feeling of being trapped crept in. *Fuck.* Any answer she gave other than "it's not different" would bring her right back to his original question. She did think she was special. "I don't function like other people do. I'll be fine. My work is too important for me to be wasting time being 'helped' when I don't need it."

"You're still a person, Elle. And no matter the type, unless you're a masochistic psychopath, you're going to have lingering effects. I get it. You are the job. Your self-image is being threatened. You had fundamental beliefs about who you are, which have been shaken. Just because you deny it, doesn't make it any less true. If you want to regain some control in your life, you need to learn to live with your new reality, because it's not going anywhere."

"What the hell does that mean?"

"It means you need to accept that underneath everything that makes you uniquely you, you're still a person who has emotions. You need to allow yourself to have emotions, and to understand them. Then, you make conscious decisions about how you are going to respond or act."

"Decision-making is not an issue for me."

"Really? So, you've been choosing denial this whole time?"

"I'm not in denial!"

"Okay. Let's test that theory. PTSD typically involves intrusive and reoccurring memories of the traumatic event, nightmares, physical reactions to something that reminds you of the trauma, changes to your ability to think clearly, uncontrollable mood swings, being easily startled, trouble sleeping, irritability, anger, and aggressive behavior. Do you have all the hallmarks of PTSD?"

Another trap. Elle jumped out of her chair. "What do you want from me? Am I supposed to cry? Scream halle-fucking-lujah? That was a complete set up, and you know it!"

"Sure, it was. And an effective one. Now you can't continue denying what's going on with you, unless you make a conscious decision to continue deluding yourself. While I highly recommend you avoid the latter option, at least that would still be progress."

Torn between screaming and crying, Elle started pacing. She felt sick. Claustrophobic. Vulnerable. She had to move; she couldn't sit back down. *Is this a panic attack?*

Wise let her pace for a few moments before asking, "What are you feeling right now?

"I feel like I'm losing my damn mind. I need to get the fuck out of here."

16

"Be more specific."

Throwing her hands up in agitation, Elle yelled, "I don't know how I feel!"

"Then focus. Right now, you're flailing. Instead of constantly being in react mode, concentrate on what's going on with you specifically. Get your brain back into the fight. Trying to force your emotions back into submission based on how you think you should be is impossible. It won't work no matter how hard you push yourself. Go at this systematically. Focus on what you're feeling, identify it, the level of intensity, and then identify why you're feeling it. If it's too much, pick one aspect to start with and work from there. You're not going to like a lot of the answers you come up with by doing this, but you need to accept them. You can't move forward if you don't."

Rationally, she couldn't see any fault with his direction. Elle crossed her arms over her chest, took a deep breath, and closed her eyes. She could feel her heart racing and her stomach churning—anxiety. She had the overwhelming urge to punch something for no reason at all. The anxiety was stronger. Why was she feeling it? Answers that came to her mind made the anxiety worse. *I'm not who I thought I was. I'm vulnerable.* Was he right?

"You will get through this," Wise said, as if he could read her emotions. "PTSD does not have to rule your life. Things may have changed for you, but how you move forward will determine whether you become stronger or continue to suffer."

Reluctantly, she returned to the chair. The anxiety was making her feel shaky and sick. "So, what happens next?"

"Hear me out. You're damaged and unstable but trying to convince everyone that you're not. That type of person does not fit the profile of a covert agent. Agency protocol does not allow someone like you to go into the field, and our top targets know that. I think you could infiltrate places we've never been because no one will ever believe you're CIA. We have a unique opportunity to use your current circumstances to our advantage. But you need to learn control."

"Control of what?"

"Yourself. You should have been able to put on whatever façade necessary to get through your recovery, but you couldn't. You're like an exposed nerve. Give me a solid week to work with you. We'll break things down and go through it all step by step until you can do it on your own. The hardest part of all this is embracing the inevitable parts you will not like and reconciling with the things that happened. You're going to be put way outside your comfort zone, and you need to let it happen. You need to allow yourself to really feel what you're going through if you have any hope of regaining control."

"Meaning?"

"It means you can't keep forcing things. You've been holding onto your emotions too tightly, afraid to let them out of the box. You need an outlet that will help you, not make things worse. It's going to take time, but, if you want to feel like you're back in control, you're going to need a new approach."

"Could you drop the psychobabble for a minute and just give it to me straight?

He let out a long sigh but kept his smile in place. "You figure out what you're feeling and why. Then, allow yourself to feel it." He held up a hand to stop her protest. "If that means crying, then cry. If it means venting anger, then find a way that isn't destructive. If it's fear, then find a way to get through it without denying it's there. Choosing how you react, and why, is critical to getting through this. If you have to scream, then scream in that moment or come up with a plan to scream at a more appropriate time. The point is, become an active participant in your life again. Even if the choices are terrible or seem minuscule, make the choice. Be proactive instead of reactive."

That sounded entirely too simple to Elle but, at the same time, it seemed feasible. She hadn't thought about trying anything like he was proposing, and that made her hesitant, but she couldn't really identify why. Pride? Ego? Did she have anything to lose at this point? She and Wise were bound by confidentiality agreements, and he seemed to get her. "So, what's the game plan?"

"Buy into sessions with me like you have with physical therapy, even if it makes you uncomfortable. This is probably going to be harder than anything else to date. You're not an idiot. So, don't fight me, and you should grasp everything. At which point, I'll make the recommendation to Calloway to clear you for duty."

Elle felt the need to move again and walked over to the window. Her mind and emotions were, once again, at war. There was no doubt she was going to go through with it, but her gut still churned in protest.

CHAPTER 3

As Elle packed up what little she had at the hospital, she couldn't keep her thoughts from drifting. Wise hadn't been overstating the strain his sessions would have on her. Elle felt more drained after her first several visits to his office than she had after any of her physical therapy workouts. Regardless of how she felt, though, she held up her end of the bargain.

For the most part.

But, true to his word, Wise cleared her to return to work. During their final session, he implored her to continue with therapy.

"You've come a long way, Elle, but you need to go further. Someone like you is at a high risk for backsliding or getting into trouble."

"Meaning…?"

"Your identity is tied to your work, so you're going to go running head first back into the thick of things. The most likely outcome is that it will bring on a barrage of memories and emotions that will make doing your job almost impossible. You may have flashbacks, and there will be physical and emotional reactions that will come on suddenly. Chances are that it will be overwhelming, and you'll end up choosing dangerous outlets."

"Well, as long as I'm choosing my outlet, I suppose that would still be progress. Right, Doc?"

"I'm serious. Be a smartass all you want, but this is no joking matter. You need to be mindful that you don't lose control again."

That sobered Elle. "I won't. That's not an option. But neither is waiting any longer. I need to get back to work or, if you thought I was hostile and uncooperative before, just wait." As she started to leave, she asked, "Why me? Other agents would kill to get cleared to return to the field."

"You pushed to get cleared. You're cleared. And now you're asking why?" Wise nearly laughed out loud.

Elle smiled for the first time in weeks. "I know. But…."

He was quiet for so long after that, Elle wasn't sure he was going to answer her.

"You said it yourself, other agents would kill for the opportunity, but would they die for it? Or more to the point, would they die without it?"

Elle felt like she'd been doused in ice water. "What are you implying?"

"No implication, Elle. Just facts. The only thing keeping you going is the drive to get back to the job. Without it, what do you think you would do?"

• • •

Elle grabbed her bag and went to the main entrance where a taxi was waiting. The drive to her residence in Arlington would take about thirty minutes depending on traffic, which gave her time to collect her thoughts.

Elle had started unraveling ISIS from within by using their own online network against them. They might have proclaimed themselves as the Islamic State but, to her, they were Daesh—a gang of delusional, bloodthirsty psychopaths who used religion to justify their actions.

Her plan started out exactly as anticipated. Elle created major divides in the group by killing some key players and making Daesh members believe their leadership was responsible for the murders. But, she had only been a fraction of the way toward her end goal, she was caught in a trap. To keep the turmoil going, her partner, Mike Traviano, *aka* Tex, had volunteered to lead a small Special Operation team in a series of surgical strikes against key members on all sides of the divide. When their progress stalled, they were forced to go in a different direction.

New ties within the organization would be forming, and Daesh would evolve into a different entity. Her window of opportunity to finish this was closing.

Thinking about Tex, Eve, and Jack steadied her resolve. When everything had gone south, they had stepped up. She needed to get back to them and see this through. Remembering the precarious position she had left them in lit the fire of her determination again.

When Elle woke up in the hospital in Germany after being medically evacuated from Iraq, her teammate, Eve James, had been there. The woman was so much more to her now than just a skilled analyst; she was the closest thing Elle had to a real friend. Eve had gathered what few personal items Elle had left at their base of operations in Baghdad and, along with her tech expert, Jack Paulson, jumped on the first flight out. They had stayed with Elle for two weeks, until she was out of the woods, at which point they returned to Iraq to assist Tex with the fallout. She hadn't spoken to any of them since. They had to maintain the security of the operation.

Arriving home, Elle paused a moment before getting out of the cab. Her house blended in seamlessly with all the others in the neighborhood, compliments of the homeowner's association rules. Usually, that was what she wanted, to avoid drawing any attention. For some reason that bothered her today. Elle paid the driver and collected her bag.

The house was exactly as she'd left it. Silence greeted her, and it made her uncomfortable. It felt empty. Rationalizing that it made sense to feel different since she'd had people around her twenty-four-seven for the last several months helped. She would adjust soon enough but, for now, it didn't matter. Getting prepped for the next stage of her mission was what mattered. She had to check in with Calloway and get back in the game.

Calloway was not someone who shied away from taking risks. You didn't head up an organization like the Central Intelligence Agency by playing it safe. But, he wasn't one to take those risks without weighing the benefits. The man was smart, experienced, and did not pull punches when it came to dealing with his operatives. Elle respected him, but she knew he was going to be scrutinizing her every move.

Calling Calloway's secretary, she asked to be scheduled immediately. At first, the secretary tried to tell her that the director was too busy to fit her in, but Elle cut her off, "You can either find some time in his schedule today, or tomorrow I'm just going to barge into whichever meeting he has first." The pause on the other end told Elle that the secretary was taking her seriously.

When the woman finally replied, she asked her to hold. When the line picked back up it was Director Calloway's voice.

"I see you still know how to make an impression, Ms. Anderson."

"Whatever it takes to get the job done, sir."

"I was told you were being released today, but I'm assuming this is not a social call to let me know that you're doing well?"

"I am doing well, sir, but you're right. I would like to come in and meet with you today."

"Normally, I would say no, but I have no doubt that you would just come anyway and camp outside my door. Since I just had a meeting cancelled this afternoon, be here in two hours, and we'll talk. But don't get too far ahead of yourself, Ms. Anderson. I know what you're going to ask. There are protocols that still need to be followed."

Elle's anger flared, but she steadied it. "I'll see you in two hours, sir. Thank you."

Putting the energy that erupted from that phone call to use, Elle went up the stairs to change for her meeting. She needed to be on her A game, which included looking the part. She had to ensure Calloway didn't have a shred of doubt that she was ready to finish the mission. Once Calloway gave the green light, everything needed to get set up for the next phase of the plan. She wanted to get back to the team as soon as possible.

• • •

Two hours later, she was standing outside of Director Calloway's office in her favorite pinstripe suit ready to do battle. The secretary threw her some sideways glances as if she were waiting for Elle to burst into the office. Elle considered doing a couple of feint moves, just to see what she would do, but decided to refrain. Instead of being shown in, Elle was surprised when the door opened, and the director came out.

He extended his hand. "Ms. Anderson, it's good to have you back."

"Thank you, sir. It's good to be back."

"Please, come in. Would you like anything? Coffee, water?"

"No, sir. I don't intend to take up too much of your time."

Calloway chuckled to himself and gestured for her to go into his office. Once he had shut the door and seated himself, they got down to business. "You were right when you predicted that the death of Muhammad Kalash would have a uniting effect on the organization. Someone is already being groomed to take his spot, and there have been ten attacks in the last week. The casualty list includes several Special Operations personnel."

"Then we need to act now, sir. Let me finish my mission."

"You're a unique asset to my directorate, Ms. Anderson, and we continue to put you in unconventional positions. Your last endeavor almost killed you. Now, we are in an unusual situation, and we are looking at an even more unconventional resolution. Sending you back into the field is a risk that I've accepted based on an assessment of target vulnerabilities and of you. But, logic dictates that we stick with protocol to the greatest extent possible to avoid another tragedy."

"I knew what I was signing up for when I accepted the position. As you said, this is an unusual situation. Conventional approaches will get us nowhere. I'm not tucking tail and running because I had a close call. The risk is worth it, sir. Let me run my operation the way I want to, and I will succeed."

A slow smile spread across Calloway's face. "Alright, Ms. Anderson. I'll give you provisional clearance to go back into the field, but I will have oversight of every move you make. If at any point I feel like you're faltering, I will pull you from the field, and there will be no going back. Is that clear?"

"Yes, sir."

CHAPTER 4

Three days later, Elle was back in Baghdad. The helicopter landed directly in the Special Operations Forces, or SOF, compound where her team had set up their base of operations. No need to be subtle, since the team wouldn't be there much longer.

It was close to sunset, so the sky had an orange cast, though there was still plenty of light. As Elle started the half-mile walk to the building with a bag slung over her shoulder, she couldn't help feeling odd about being back.

The compound was bustling with activity. Checking her watch, she estimated that it was close to shift change. It wasn't the best time for her to arrive since she wanted to avoid drawing attention, and a helicopter is hard to miss. She felt the eyes on her as she walked, and her skin crawled. Pressing on as though her arrival was nothing of consequence, she reminded herself that she chose this course of action because speed was more important now than stealth. Time was slipping away.

It looked like the area had been hammered with rain shortly before she arrived; everything was soaked. She made sure to watch her footing to avoid straying from the gravel pathways. Like moon dust, the sand was so fine it turned into a slick paste when it was wet. The temperature was starting to drop with the setting sun, but the rain had kicked up the humidity, and Elle could feel her clothes and hair sticking to her skin. Moving with purpose, she was back in front of her Baghdad base of operations in no time. The small, wooden building had served them well. Initially, her team was only supposed to be there a few weeks, but it had been months. Guilt hit her, and she had to force herself to go inside.

She walked through the main entryway doors and saw that all the alcoves along the far wall had been cleared, and several pelican cases and kit bags were now stacked there. Her team had been busy packing up in preparation for the move. Elle hadn't spoken to them yet, although she had sent instructions ahead of time. Her pulse was racing, and she felt queasy. Elle set down her bag and took several deep breaths to settle herself. She couldn't understand why she was so nervous. This was her team, and she had a job to do—it should be that simple. The butterflies in her stomach held her in place.

Would she see pity in their eyes? Would they judge her or reject her return?

There was only one way to find out.

Forcing one foot in front of the other, Elle went into the Operations center. She could hear pop music playing, which meant Eve was there. The room was in disarray with partially packed cases, and Eve and Jack, working away. But they were so intent on their task that Elle stood there a moment just watching before either one noticed. Jack turned and almost ran into her, letting out a girly squeal of surprise. "You almost gave me a heart attack, Elle. Can't you just say hi like a normal person? Or better yet, wear a damn bell so we can hear you coming?"

Laughing, Elle said, "I'll take it under advisement, Jack."

Eve launched herself at Elle. She barely braced herself in time for the impact.

"I missed you, too, Eve." Her anxiety eased thanks to her friend's warm welcome, and she found herself breathing easier. Carefully, she started to extricate herself from the hug and took a good look at her team. Both looked healthy but worn. They had obviously been working long, hard hours. Jack looked paler than usual, and Eve seemed to have lost a little weight. The guilt she felt earlier started to creep back in, but she held it at bay despite doctor's orders of letting these emotions pass through.

"Are you guys okay? It looks like you've been busy. What's been going on?"

"We didn't think you would be coming back, Elle," Eve said.

"The job isn't over. Before you ask, I'm fine. But time is something we don't have. Fill me in."

Eve's lips pressed together tightly, but she did as Elle asked. "It was hard without you. But we stuck with the plan as long as we could. After you removed our first few targets and made it look like it was carried out by the Daesh leadership, the organization fractured. We targeted key personnel in the rival factions to keep the infighting going, and it was working like a charm. The infighting made it possible for the Coalition Forces to win back a lot of territories and drive Daesh back. But then things started to change. It got harder to identify and find targets that would keep the internal strife going. Some of the groups merged, and others have gone silent. Nothing we did had an impact anymore."

"That's when I stepped in," Jack said. "I used the online access we hijacked after you killed their cyber leads to try and stir things up again, but the response wasn't anything of significance."

"I figured that would happen. We're going to be 'wheels up' first thing tomorrow, so make sure you're ready to go. We'll have plenty of time to talk later, but for now, let's focus on getting out of here." Elle felt a presence behind her, and she turned.

"It's about damn time, Mama."

Tears welled up in her eyes. Without conscious thought, she threw her arms around Tex. She could feel his muscles tighten in shock before he returned the hug. She trembled from the force of her emotions, and it embarrassed her that she couldn't stop, but she didn't fight it. Tex had saved her life. He had pushed her to accept him as a full partner, a title he more than lived up to. Words were failing her, but she managed a weak, "Thank you."

"Hey, I was just returning the favor. Besides, I didn't want to have to break in another team lead." Tex was trying to make light of the situation, but the crack in his voice gave him away.

Elle had saved his life shortly after they'd met. He had taken the lead on a mission, thinking it would be a walk in the park. It wasn't. It had been a setup, and Tex would have been killed, but Elle got to him first. That was nothing compared to what he had done for her. Tex had defied orders, and all the odds, to not only extract her from her captors but also to get her the medical treatment she needed just in time to bring her back from the brink. Then, he had called in favors and made sacrifices to try to keep her operation on track. She knew Calloway had pushed him to take over, but he held his ground. They all had. It would have been easier to just follow orders without question. Still, they had developed a complementary plan and ran with it while they waited it out. That's loyalty.

Pulling back from the embrace, Elle got a good look at Tex and didn't like what she saw. The dark circles under his eyes enhanced the new scar on the right side of his face. It looked like something sharp had carved a line from his temple to his cheekbone. He was thinner, and she could see a few grey hairs that hadn't been there before. Everything protective in her leaped to the forefront.

"What's been going on, Tex?"

He let out a long sigh. "I suppose it's about time you got down to business."

Elle's mouth quirked up in a smile, but she didn't rise to the bait.

"Fine. Take a seat, and we'll give you the down and dirty. Eve has already prepped some files for you to review, as well as updates to the original target folders."

Eve retrieved several folders from a messenger bag and brought them to Elle.

"For the first few weeks, we worked on targets that the SOF guys were already tracking within Daesh that fit the mold we needed to keep their little civil war going. Since the SOF targeting process takes longer than ours does, we just went with the flow to buy more time. After a month, we had to adjust our tactics to show progress to the higher-ups. The missions did not have the impact they wanted, so Calloway put us under the control of one of the senior Operations Officers, John Baker. Good guy, lots of experience in the region, but he runs pretty standard operations. Identify and eliminate key players. All in total, we've done about fifteen missions in the last few months. But they've taken a lot of effort to execute—4 was the first key player on our original list. When Baker ordered us to take him out, I requested that we find a way to use him to subvert the network's momentum. The best he could come up with was to push the Iraqi involvement. His rationale was to show that fellow Muslims were fighting against these guys, to highlight that this isn't about religion. Sound logic, but only on paper. The mission went like clockwork, but the second and third-order effects were not what anyone was hoping for."

Elle took some time to flip through the folders of the various targets to get some more background. Each individual was low-level but connected to emergent voices or key facilitators on each side of the organization's divide. As she skimmed through the data, she saw the Syrian leadership was consolidating power.

She felt anger building.

Mahmud Hussein, Number 3. Elle wanted to go after that man now, but that was making things personal, and that wasn't what needed to happen next. Forcing herself to focus on her overall mission, Elle reviewed the updates to her original target list.

1—Khalid Omar (Imam/Baghdad): Deceased

2—Muhammad Walid (Imam/Syria): Current location Raqqa

3—Mahmud Hussein (Cleric/Syria): Current location Raqqa (likely wounded)

4—Muhammad Kalash (Cleric/Mosul): Deceased

5—Uday Satar (Cleric/Al Anbar): Deceased

6—Hans Waite (Banker/ Geneva): Current location Rome, Italy

7—Gerard Fior (Black Market/Djibouti): Based out of the Kempinski Hotel

8—Sallah Huway (Hwallah/Al-Qaim): Deceased

9—Victor Morrow (Film/Mosul): Deceased

10—Rami Hasar (Cyber/Baghdad): Deceased

11—Mufti Assan (Cyber/Baghdad): Deceased

"What happened to Number 9?" Elle asked.

"He was taken out in an airstrike about two months ago, which is why you haven't seen much more than amateur footage of their attacks lately and nothing from the senior leadership.

Elle frowned at the missed opportunity, but she wasn't going to waste time dwelling. From the beginning, she'd planned on taking out the moneymen first but had been ordered to deviate. No more. To have any hope of dismantling Daesh, they had to cut off critical support lines, and she had already set things into motion. "Keep packing as planned. We're going to need a smaller footprint in our next location, so only take the minimum gear you need to operate in Djibouti. I have a suite already lined up. We need to look like we have a lot of money. With the level of corruption, the only thing that will get us what we need is to stand out among the country's wealthiest. So, break out your most expensive attire and ditch the 5.11 cargo pants and collared shirts."

"How can we help?" A man behind her asked.

Elle whipped around toward the familiar male voice. Her heart skipped a beat when she saw Julian standing in the doorway. Julian, beauty, brains, and a real asset to the team. Smiling, she was just about to answer him when another man came into view. Red Shirt. Since both men had already been exposed to her team's operations, when Tex needed backup, he had called them. She'd hoped to never see the trigger-happy, sexist, sociopath again. His real name was Robert something. Her stomach lurched at the sight of him standing in her Ops center.

"Gentlemen. Please, come in and sit down. We have a long-overdue conversation to have."

Julian obliged her without any hesitation, but Red Shirt sauntered around the room until he perched on the corner of the desk closest to Eve. He made a show of looking impatient, like he was humoring her.

Ignoring the act, Elle directed her remarks to Julian. "I want to start by thanking you for backing Tex when he came for me and for watching his six ever since.

We're not a conventional unit. But pulling you guys in like we did was unconventional…even for us. Now that you're here, you have a choice to make. Most of what you've seen has been the type of mission you're accustomed to. From here on out, that changes."

"And why is that?" Red Shirt asked.

"Because we're getting back on task, and a military approach will not be useful. There will come a time for it later but not now."

"What does that mean for us?" Julian asked.

"That's up to you. I need my primary team operating in its usual construct, and there's no time for training. If you stay on for this next phase, it will be in a support and assist capacity. You'll take your orders from me."

"I don't know who you think you are, sweetheart, but you're getting ahead of yourself. I've saved your ass twice now, so you don't get to order me around."

Elle was on her feet and in Red Shirt's face in seconds. "Let me be clear. This is my team and my operation. You provided assistance, and I thanked you for it. As of this moment, you get in line, or you get the fuck out."

Red Shirt jumped off the desk, towering over her. Elle didn't need to turn around to know that Tex and Julian lined up behind her. She could feel them there. Irritated, she started to react, but Tex put a restraining hand on her shoulder.

"You knew the deal, Robert. Elle is our lead, and it's her call. Period. You can quit and go back to your unit if you can't handle it, but those are your only choices."

Elle watched as Red Shirt ran through options in his mind before his gaze returned to her. Hatred burned there. She was ready for him to attack, and she dared him with her eyes to do it.

"Fine. If G.I. Jane here is in charge, you'll need me to stick around." Elle saw the promise of retaliation in his expression. If it hadn't been for Tex's hold on her, she would have attacked him. But then Red Shirt returned to the desk by Eve.

Yanking her shoulder out of Tex's grip, she walked to her bag and snatched out six large envelopes.

As she handed one to Tex, he whispered, "You good? I've never seen you spin up so fast."

"He should have never been here in the first place," Elle replied.

"It's a little late for blame. It's done. He's here."

He was right, and she knew it, but she was still angry. Walking around the room, she handed each member of her team an envelope. When she got to Julian, she asked, "What about you? Are you staying?"

"If you'll have me, I'm in. I don't mind grunt work, and I would like to see this through. Besides, the conventional stuff gets boring after a while."

Elle searched his face to see if he was sincere. She still couldn't get a read on him, but her gut told her he could be trusted. "Okay. In each envelope is your new cover identification. Since this is new to most of you, we kept things as close to reality as possible. First names and the amount of time you've been with this team remain the same. I'm an ex-spook who started this group four years ago when I recruited Mike after leaving Special Forces. We stole Jack and Eve from the private sector almost a year ago. And you two are ex-military recently brought on as extra muscle."

"What's going on, Elle?" Eve asked. Jack looked pale.

"We're going into Djibouti as a team of high-priced mercenaries. I've made sure that these identities have been linked to various unattributed events around the world. None of the links are direct but should jump out at anyone who knows what they are doing. Any background checks on us will lead to the conclusion that we're serious players, and professional enough to have avoided being directly implicated."

"None of them have been trained for this, Elle," Tex said.

"Come on, not like it's hard," Red Shirt replied.

Elle didn't acknowledge the outburst. "The covers are part of the illusion, Tex. And they need something to draw from for any interactions we have to keep from tripping alarms. You and I will be doing the heavy lifting."

"So, what's next?" Julian asked.

"Now that I know you and Robert are staying, you will be taking over security and logistics. Tex, you and I need to pack up our weapons loadout. I've already made arrangements for new gear. We're going to lock up whatever we don't need for the next phase and leave it here on the compound. Eve, I'll need everything you've got on Number 7. Jack, I know you want to take all your toys, but we need a smaller signature for our next two locations. Bring only your favorites. You're going to need to cart it around through a civilian airport, so pack light and avoid pelican cases to lower our profile. Remember, tomorrow we're high-paid mercs, so dress the part. Time is short, so we'll work out details on the plane. Our flight is scheduled for the morning, so let's move."

Elle left and went to their small armory and prep room. Most everything had been packed up except the weapons. The cases were neatly stacked in spots that corresponded to where items had been laid out previously. Grabbing her weapons case, Elle paused when she saw her rifle. Vivid images of the last time she had the M4 flashed through her head. She was on the roof being ambushed, and then she was fighting her way out of captivity. Sweat broke out across her body, and her hands trembled. Her pulse raced out of control. Closing her eyes and leaning on the table for balance, she tried to calm her breathing. These were just memories. She had survived and moved past this. She needed to get a grip.

"Elle?"

Tex's voice startled her, and she jumped. His eyebrows furrowed at her reaction, but he didn't comment. Julian was standing beside him. "We're heading out. Eve and Jack are going to chow. Robert and I will get the CONEX boxes prepped, and I've asked Julian to help finish packing up in here. Did you need anything?"

"I'm good, Tex. Thanks," she answered, forcing herself to look at ease.

Tex nodded and left. Elle put on a smile for Julian, but she still felt shaky and the images burned in her mind. *Find a distraction.* "So, we meet again."

He held out his hand and said, "Julian Saunders. Chief Petty Officer, SEAL. Reporting for duty, ma'am."

Chuckling, Elle shook his hand. "Elle Anderson. Special Team Lead, Central Intelligence Agency. And you can drop the ma'am bullshit, Elle is fine." She could still feel the warmth of his hand on hers as she sat down and kicked out a chair for him. Julian took the hint and sat down.

"I was serious when I said that the jobs would be support and assist. A lot of the tasks will be menial for someone with your skillset. I won't be offended if you bow out."

"I appreciate you being straight with me, but I meant what I said. I don't mind being the support guy. I may have only seen a piece of the puzzle, but it's been obvious to me from the moment I met you that something big was happening."

From the moment they met, she couldn't deny her interest or attraction to Julian. But it was more than that. She felt something whenever she was near him, and that never happened to her. *Focus.*

"Tell me what I need to know about you, Julian."

"Well, I joined the Navy after 9/11. Never thought about the military before then. But that day I realized I was patriotic and really pissed off. So, I enlisted. The SEALs just seemed to be the best fit. Since then, I've been all over the world, doing things that most only get to see in the movies or read about in books. I'm an only child, never been married, and have no kids. Unless you count my dogs. I'm a Virgo, my favorite color is blue, and I hate brussels sprouts."

Elle laughed. "Seems odd to be having this conversation after everything we've been through already. But, I suppose it's better late than never. I don't trust people easily, but knowing you had Tex's back kept me from losing my mind during recovery. I can't thank you enough for that."

"You don't have to. It's my job."

Elle felt a pang of desire. "You always seem to know exactly what to say to me."

"I heard you say it was off to Djibouti next. So, I guess that means Gerard Fior is the next target?"

Case in point. "Yes, but we don't use the names after they're identified. Just the number."

"Why is that?"

"They're a task to be completed. Nothing else."

"I can understand that. Provides distance."

"What else do you need to know?"

"I don't need to know anything else right now. I've seen you take a bullet. And I was there after your capture. I saw what they did to you, but you weren't going down without a fight. Despite everything that happened, you came back. That tells me more than anything else ever could. You're the real deal."

Elle's chest tightened. Being back here churned up so many emotions. Before she could stop herself, she was out of her chair and on Julian's lap. His body tensed in surprise. But, just like before, flames leaped the moment they touched. She kissed him forcefully, and he succumbed to the fire. As she pulled Julian's shirt over his head, Wise lecturing her about dangerous outlets for PTSD flashed through her mind. She hesitated and felt her anxiety surge. But as his hands roamed her body, her mind relented.

Elle stood and grabbed Julian's waistband, pulling him up with her. Julian followed her movement and pushed her back into the nearest wall, relieving her of her shirt. Every nerve in her body felt alive, electric. It was liberating. She had to force herself to move them to her room in the back.

Once they reached the little partition that had served as her room, Julian lifted her, and she wrapped her legs around his waist. He put a knee on the bed and lowered her to the mattress, keeping full contact with her body the entire time. Every move was commanding. His touch worshipped her body hungrily, like he couldn't get enough.

Shedding the rest of their clothes, Elle rode a tide of sensation that drove everything else away.

CHAPTER 5

Elle lay in Julian's arms, relishing the way her body felt. Her skin was sensitive to the touch, and her heart was still pounding, but it was slowing down as she caught her breath. She ran her fingers absent-mindedly across the arm he had draped over her torso as he lay beside her. His arm moved, and his fingers ran over her skin almost reverently. She closed her eyes and enjoyed the feeling until his fingers ran over the scar on her left side. Instantly, she tensed and pushed his hand away. Sitting up, Elle avoided looking at him and grabbed for her clothes.

"Memories too close?" Julian asked.

Elle froze, surprised by his perception. As soon as she wasn't wrapped up in sex, her brain started firing on all cylinders, and she was reliving the impact of the bullet. Wanting to fall back into the passion that drove everything else away, Elle crawled on top of him. But

Julian just kissed her and held her close. Eventually, she relaxed, listening to the steady rhythm of his heartbeat.

The moment was broken by the sound of a closing door.

The partition next to her was where Eve slept. She felt exposed. Her personal life was not something she shared with anyone, ever.

Julian must have noticed the change in her. "Breathe, Elle. However you want to play this, I'll follow your lead. One way or the other, I'm still in." Grinning, he added, "If the position of cabana boy is open, I'd like to submit my résumé."

His quip cut through her nerves. "I appreciate that." Getting to her feet, she continued dressing. The second she remembered where she left her shirt, she looked outside of her room. Eve had neatly folded both their shirts and laid them on the desk in the corner. *Well, shit.* Sighing deeply, she retrieved the garments and handed Julian his shirt.

Once they were both dressed, Julian yanked her into his arms and covered her mouth in a passionate kiss. Then, he pulled back and said, "If it wasn't obvious by now, I'm very attracted to you, Elle. But I didn't volunteer to stay so I could get you into bed. I'm on your team, and I've got your back no matter what you decide."

Elle just looked at him for a while. What the hell was she going to do now? Rationally, this man was an asset, and she should take full advantage of having his skills at her disposal. But he was dangerous to her. She couldn't afford any more distractions than she already had. It was hard enough to focus without their attraction complicating matters. "No promises. We'll try things with you on the team for now. But if it doesn't work, then the mission is going to come first."

"I'd expect nothing less."

Walking over to the Ops center, they found the rest of the team. Elle thought she would see disappointment or admonishment, but everyone seemed okay. Except for Eve, who looked delighted. And Red Shirt, who sneered at her. *Fuck.* There was still packing left to do, and her team was in the middle of pulling the monitors down. She moved to help them finish.

Pre-staging her equipment with her bags, Elle took a few moments to lay out everything she needed in the morning and re-pack the remaining items. She checked all her weapons and placed them in her custom case. Their weapons cases would be packed away, and if everything went according to plan, they would have new gear waiting for them at the hotel. All the right bribes had already been paid. She did not anticipate any issues at the airport in Djibouti City, other than the usual. Corruption is a way of life throughout most of Africa. Djibouti was no exception.

Sitting on her bed, Elle ran through the dossier on Number 7 again, studying his picture and what reporting they had on this man. Tomorrow, she would begin another game. For the first time there was comfort in knowing that this mission would require her to play a specific role. It had all just been part of the job before—but she needed to lose herself in a character this time.

She could hear Eve packing, so she went over. "You need help with anything, kid?"

"I'm almost done. Just trying to decide which outfit makes me look the part of a mercenary more."

Elle stifled a laugh. Eve would never pull off that look, but she didn't have to. She just needed to look wealthy. Eve had laid out every piece of black clothing that she had, so Elle started by gathering them up. "First of all, you've been watching too many movies. Second, where we're going, it's ungodly hot. You're not wearing these heavy suits."

"But I don't have anything else that will work."

Shaking her head, Elle opened the garment bag hanging on the wall and pulled out the empty hangers. As she did, she noticed a couple of dresses and a linen pantsuit were still hanging inside. Pulling those items out, Elle laid them across the bed to get a better look. Weighing those options, she chose the pantsuit. "Wear this with a camisole, heels, and jewelry."

"It's white. Isn't that going to make me stand out?"

"We want to stand out, to project that we're in the game. Professionals. To do that, you need to look like you're used to being well paid."

"Oh, alright. This look is more my style, anyway."

Eve's bubbly personality was back in full swing as the two of them put away the rest of her clothing. She did most of the talking, reminiscing about where she got the different pieces she had. Eventually, though, she came around to what Elle knew she was dying to talk about.

"So, how long have you and Julian been a thing?"

"We're not a thing. He and I just have chemistry, nothing more."

Eve's face was almost comical as she rolled her eyes. "Nothing more, my ass."

Elle laughed out loud and felt some tension drain away. "We talked about clothes and accessories, and now it's boys? Should we put on our pajamas and have a pillow fight next?"

"If I have to resort to beating you with a pillow until you talk about Julian, I will."

Smiling, Elle said, "I'm going to do one last walkthrough. Get some sleep; we've got an early day tomorrow."

As she walked away, Eve called after her, "He's a good one, Elle. And you deserve to have someone. Don't fight it. Besides, if he hurts you, I'll kick his butt."

At a loss of how to respond, she simply said, "Good night, Eve."

Somehow the building felt smaller with all the gear packed up. It was easy to see that they were as ready as they were going to be. Checking the alcoves by the entrance to their building, Elle could hear someone talking outside.

Opening the door, she heard Red Shirt on a cell phone. "...typical equal opportunity bullshit. The woman has no idea what the hell she's doing, just looking to bang team guys."

"What do you think you're doing?" Elle interrupted.

"None of your fucking business," he snarled.

"Give me the phone or you're done. You're compromising this mission."

"Let me call you back." Red Shirt hung up. "You don't get to tell me what to do."

"Actually, that's exactly what I get to do. It's my team and my lead. If you have a problem, then fucking leave."

"You'd love that, wouldn't you? I'm the only one who sees through your shit. You want to talk about being compromised? I bet your boss would love to hear how great of a leader you are. Particularly how comfortable you've gotten with the help."

Elle didn't respond. Every muscle in her body coiled up to strike, both hands balled into fists. *Say one more thing.*

Looking victorious, Red Shirt turned and sauntered away. Pulling the phone back out, she could hear his laughter echo as he returned to his call. Elle wanted blood. Fighting the urge to chase him down, she walked in the opposite direction. She needed to move, anger seething in her mind like a living thing. *If you lose it, he wins.* He was too savvy to say anything genuinely compromising. It would be her word against his. No matter the outcome, if Red Shirt opened his mouth, there was no doubt that Calloway would see it as a reason to remove her from the field. She couldn't let that happen. It grated on Elle that Red Shirt felt like he could hold anything over her, but it was secondary to her need to get back to work. She would deal with him eventually, one way or the other.

CHAPTER 6

Elle woke up with a start, trembling violently as the remnants of the dream continued to exert its force on her. Sitting up, she wiped her face with her shirtsleeve and tried to get under control. She was covered with sweat and crying. Her heart was pounding so loud she had to strain to listen for any telltale signs that she had awakened Eve.

Silence greeted her. At first, she was relieved. It was quiet. Too quiet. The adrenaline of the nightmare propelled her from her bed to Eve's room. Eve was fast asleep. The relief actually made Elle feel faint. She took a few minutes to steady her nerves and then returned to her room. There was no way she was going to be able to sleep anymore. Checking the time, she saw it was less than an hour from when she intended to wake up anyway.

Grabbing her stuff, she headed for the bathroom but stopped when she saw Tex sitting in the Ops center working on a laptop.

"Good morning," he said

"What are you doing?" she asked.

"Just double-checking that everything is set. Robert has a bad habit of cutting corners, and I want our first mission back together to go smooth."

"The first chance I get to be rid of him, I'm taking it." Silence followed that comment. Elle did not like the look on his face.

"You know I need to ask, so don't read into it, but are you ready for this?"

She wanted to lash out but refrained. "Ready or not, I need to be here."

"Not going to lie, Elle, I'm worried about you. Robert is a piece of shit, but I've never seen you lose your cool so quickly. And Julian is about as stand up as a guy can be, but this is so far outside of the way you normally act. It's like you're a totally different person." Tex moved to stand directly across from her and waited until she looked up at him. "We need you fully engaged if we're going to make it through this. If you're not there, then you need to learn to lean on me. Otherwise, we're screwed."

"And what if I bring you down with me?"

"That's a risk I'm ready to take. Now we've got work to do. Are you ready?"

"It's the only thing I know I'm ready for."

"Fair enough." He started to leave but turned back to her and said, "If you ever want to talk to someone who understands, Elle, I'm here." As he walked out, she thought about when Tex was the one who ended up captured and could have lost his life. Badly injured during an ambush, he was held for several hours and was moments away from a bullet when she had pulled him out. It may not have been as extreme as her own, but the similarities couldn't be ignored either. She found some comfort in seeing how he had recovered from the ordeal.

• • •

Two hours later, they were all at the airfield waiting for their private plane to get clearance to taxi for takeoff. Elle and her team had transformed themselves into their new characters. Tex somehow managed to look both debonair and intimidating in a dark-gray, pinstripe suit. Jack pulled off the image of a wealthy entrepreneur in his perfectly tailored shirt and navy slacks. Eve looked elegant and beautiful in the white, linen suit. Elle dressed in a blood-red suit that hugged her curves like a second skin. She left her hair loose around her shoulders. There was no doubt that she would draw every eye, and they would all think the same thing: dangerous.

The two newest team members hadn't been prepared for an operation like this when they had deployed with their unit, so they did the next best thing. They wore the best civilian attire they had, and they didn't shave. Even casually dressed, they screamed special operations. It fit their cover story as the newest recruits to their team.

Once they were in the air, Elle briefed them on the next part of their mission. "Before I arrived, I used a deep-cover asset to set up a buy from Number 7. The deal was accepted, payment was made over the dark web, and the weapons should be waiting for us in our suite. From the moment we set this up, he would have started pulling information on our cover IDs. By now, he has our covers as freelance mercenaries. He will assume that we were hired to do a job in DJ, so we'll be scrutinized to determine if we're a threat or the competition. He's easily the most well-trained and dangerous target on our list. From the moment we hit the ground, it's showtime. There are eyes everywhere in Djibouti City, and they are all for hire. Most of those eyes report back directly to the government officials who pull their strings, but they will report to anyone who pays them. If anyone asks why we are there, tell them you're on vacation. No one will ever believe it, but that doesn't matter. We want the intrigue. Questions so far?"

Everyone shook their head.

"Once we clear border control, we need to retrieve our bags immediately. There will be men there who will try and take them and demand payment for a bag service. Don't pay them. Stay in character. Do not say thank you. Ignore them."

"Won't that offend the locals?" Eve asked.

"No, this is normal for them. And, remember, you need to project that you are above them. We're making statements with everything we do. We need to make sure that our target sees us as players in an illicit world and being polite to the hustlers at the airport won't get you far."

Tex patted Eve's shoulder. "Don't worry. Once you see what they do, you won't feel so bad. It's just like Elle said. The Djiboutian will literally crowd the conveyer belt in baggage claim, so it's hard to get to your bags before they do. And then they just pull bags off onto the floor and try to get you to pay them. Some of them will try to sequester your bags and put them on carts to bully you into paying them to take your bags out of the airport. People fall for it all the time."

Eve nodded her understanding.

Elle continued. "Once we leave the airport, there will be a vehicle waiting. We will be heading straight to the hotel. We will have a five-room suite, and we need to make sure we do a sweep before we settle in. Jack, as soon as we get into the room, I need you to scan for bugs. The rest of us need to search for cameras. Keep the conversation to observations of the room and the country but move decisively. If anyone is watching, I want them to see an experienced group who is security focused. Start your search around outlets and anything that draws power. They'll want to watch or listen live, and avoid using equipment they have to gain access to the room to recover regularly. They would want to tap into the electricity to avoid bulky battery packs. If you find something, call it out calmly as if this happens all the time."

"I'll be able to find anything active, but then what? Do you want me to trace it?" Jack asked.

"No. Just make sure the room is clean. We'll have to check it regularly to make sure we stay that way. Leave the rest to me."

"Maybe I misunderstood this part, but I think you said five rooms. In case you can't count, there are six of us," Red Shirt said.

"You and Julian will be hot racking or sleeping on a couch, your choice. And, the two of you will be splitting watches, so someone can keep an eye on the suite and be on standby at all times," Elle said.

"You've got to be kidding me."

"Logistics and security, that's your role. I was very clear. The suite is for the job, not for your personal use. If you can't handle it, quit," Elle replied.

"I see how it is, make the new guys do the shit tasks while the rest of you live it up."

Elle didn't respond; she looked him in the eye and waited.

Finally, he said, "Whatever. Just get on with it."

"So, how do you see this going down?" Tex asked.

"We need insider access, so I'm going to find a way to get it. After we get settled, I want everyone to rest. It's going to be a late night. Everything we have on Number 7 shows that he plays hard and enjoys indulging in the nightlife. He's a regular at the Sky Bar at the top of our hotel, so we'll start there."

"You had me at Sky Bar," Tex quipped.

"You and I will take the lead and get a feel for the situation. Jack, get set up in the room as quickly as possible, so you can join us. But I want our own security in place to back Julian and Robert. If anyone attempts a surreptitious entry, I want to know about it. Eve, I know deception isn't your strong suit, but do you think you can handle it?"

"I have no idea what to say to these people, but, yeah, and I could definitely use a drink after the last few months."

"Keep it to flirting and small talk. Leave everyone wanting more. Any references to what you do for a living needs to be kept vague. Remember, you're a specialist and highly paid for your talents."

"So, close to reality except for the highly paid part," Jack added, grinning.

"This is going to take time, so I need everyone to stay focused. We can't slip up. Tex and I will take on the bulk of the interactions with these guys, but if the rest of you aren't ever around, that will be suspicious. Keep your interactions to what you think you can handle. Tex or I will pull you guys out at any time if you feel like you're in over your head. One way or the other, we need to figure out how Number 7 runs his business. It does us no good to take him out just to have his associates pick right back up and fill the void. We're going to destroy this link to Daesh."

Elle sat back and surveyed her team. She hated that Red Shirt was there, but otherwise, they looked ready. Was she?

Taking a deep breath, Elle leaned back in her seat and tried to relax. In a few hours, they would be landing, and it would be game on.

Before she knew it, they were on approach to land. Startled awake by the captain's voice, Elle looked around and saw that they had all drifted off to sleep. *The calm before the storm.* As they gathered themselves, Elle asked, "Everyone ready? Any final questions?"

"I'm looking forward to some more sleep and getting out of this suit. Otherwise, I'm good," Tex replied.

"This linen wrinkled a little more than I thought it would, but I suppose that's to be expected on an airplane," Eve said as she fussed with her jacket.

"You look great. You all do. I barely recognize you, Jack. Except for the Spider-Man socks."

He blushed and tugged at his pant legs. "They match…kinda."

Once they touched down, they were all focused and ready to go. The plane taxied for a few minutes, and then they pulled up to the end of the terminal.

Once the plane stopped, Elle watched several baggage handlers run to the aircraft. When the cabin door opened, she was assailed by the heat and smell of Djibouti. Her stomach turned a little. Elle picked up the small bag that held money and her passport and led the way off the plane. As soon as she stepped outside, the heat and the smell intensified. She had never smelled anything worse than this place. The only way to describe it was shit and despair. It made Iraq seem like nothing.

The terminal looked more like a small regional airport than the main airport for its capital city. It wasn't in the best shape, but by Djibouti standards, it was pristine. They walked in the customs area, a square room directly off the tarmac that had a serpentine rope line leading up to four desks. Only two of those desks were currently manned since they appeared to be the only flight arriving at the moment. Instead of walking through the rope maze, Elle boldly walked through the VIP lane and raised an eyebrow at the security guard in a silent challenge. She could see uncertainty pass over his features before he gestured for her to approach the first open border control agent.

Elle handed her passport to the agent and waited stoically for him to scan the document. They were each using passports that had an alias, but the documents were genuine. She did not anticipate any issues getting through customs as long as her companions didn't get nervous and make security suspicious.

"Are you here for business or pleasure?" The man asked her in heavily accented English.

"A little of both."

He held her passport up, so he could compare her face to the picture. Elle noticed his gaze dropped to her cleavage before he took one last look at the screen. Then, he stamped the selected page and waved her on without a second glance, already moving on to Eve. Jack was through, and the two of them waited together. Elle did not like the looks that Eve was getting from the security guard—or Red Shirt for that matter—but she seemed to be in control.

"Easy, Elle. She's fine."

Her knuckles were burning, and she realized that she had been making tight fists. Relaxing her hands, she lifted her chin and stared coolly at both men. Eventually, the security guard noticed her staring and visibly reacted to it. This country had a long history of class and clan divides, and, in most cases, money meant power. Elle's icy demeanor had instantly reminded him of his place, and suddenly, he was looking anywhere but at them.

Red Shirt, on the other hand, smirked when she caught his eye. *Touch her and die, motherfucker.*

Once they were all through customs, they moved to the small baggage claim area. Just as Elle had predicted, their bags had already been pulled off the conveyor belts. A scrawny, angry-looking man was standing guard next to them. As soon as they approached, he held out his hand to ask for money, but Tex waved him off.

The man backed off with a grumble but did not argue.

They picked up their luggage and walked out the door to the front of the airport.

Barricades kept vehicles from pulling up to the curb, and there was a dirt and gravel parking lot across the road. On the side of the road just outside the parking lot was a large black limousine. The driver was waiting outside of the vehicle with a sign that read *Alexander*, Elle's new last name. Walking straight to the limo and identifying herself, the driver jumped into motion, helping them load their things.

And they were on the move again.

CHAPTER 7

Driving in Djibouti City is an experience in itself. While there aren't too many vehicles on the road, they still manage to cause trouble. The main roads tend to be wide enough for four lanes, but there are no lines. Cars weave through all lanes of traffic to pass slower vehicles.

As their driver navigated this strange game of vehicular *Frogger*, Elle watched the surroundings. Things seemed to have gotten worse from the last time she had been in Djibouti, and that was saying something. The whole place seemed to be coated in a layer of dirt. The locals pieced together fences from whatever they could find, and buildings were falling apart. Their driver took them through the "nice" part of town, but proof of absolute poverty was all around them. Every so often, there would be a row of buildings or a small compound that looked more well-kept than others, but then there were massive shards of glass lining the top of the security wall, a vicious defense to keep people out, which made the place feel even less hospitable.

They passed a man lying on the side of the road on a piece of cardboard. He didn't have a shirt or shoes, and he was so skinny he looked close to death. With one leg kicked out into the street, he just stared straight ahead propped up on his elbows, leaning on the curb, disrupting traffic and tempting fate.

"Should we call someone to help him?" Eve asked.

"The only help he'll accept is for someone to give him a fix," Elle replied.

"Just because he's on the street doesn't make him a drug addict, Elle." Eve sounded offended.

Keeping her voice low so the driver couldn't hear the conversation, Elle said, "You don't understand, Eve, I'm not being judgmental. It's a way of life here. Most of the population is high on a drug called khat all the time. Even the police."

Eve looked doubtful.

"Since we're going to be working here for a bit, you need to understand some hard truths about this place. You can't trust anyone."

Eve nodded but didn't look convinced.

"It is what it is, Eve. Don't let your emotions get the better of you. If you need proof, look ahead."

They were approaching a business area of sorts. There were lines of drab, rundown buildings that housed various shops and restaurants, but all the activity was concentrated in front of the small kiosks on the street corners and interspersed between the shops. At first glance, several signs had what appeared to be hand-drawn vegetables, most very poorly done, that looked a little like leafy broccoli or asparagus. Elle watched Eve's face. She knew the moment Eve realized the signs were actually menus for different amounts of khat priced out using pictures to illustrate the amounts available for the illiterate population.

As they drove through the area, activity picked up significantly. Where things had seemed desolate before, there was now a bustle of activity, all centered on the khat sellers. Eve took in the surroundings, and the frown on her face deepened as she saw evidence of what Elle had been telling her. People who seemed to be from all walks of life were in line at the khat stands. Men in police or military uniforms, women with children in tow, and some even had babies in their arms.

"The leaves are what they want, so the first people in line will get the best cuts. But they will sell the stems to those who either don't have enough money or who showed up too late and are desperate for even a slight buzz. My last deployment was in Somalia. Khat is a thing there, too," Julian added.

"What you need to remember, Eve, is that addicts will do anything for their next fix. You can't trust the locals," Tex said.

Glancing over to Jack, Elle noticed that he seemed just as disturbed as Eve. There was a hint of disgust in his eyes, and his lips were pressed together in a thin line. "We'll be at the hotel soon. Djibouti City isn't big."

Jack met her eyes and nodded.

As they continued, the road narrowed, and the buildings gave way to more compounds. The fences were nicer, and the structures in much better repair. They started to see flags for different nations flying inside on even larger buildings. Elle said, "This is the diplomatic area. This is where the Embassies and Consulates are located. Most countries have an 'Embassy Row.' DJ isn't any different."

Lowering her voice again, Eve asked, "Won't there be a lot of security around here? Shouldn't we stay as far away as possible?"

"We need to be seen. We need to damn near strut and make sure everyone who matters sees that we have no fear of the authorities and have money to burn. A low profile will hurt us more than help us."

Tex ran his fingers through his hair. "When you're this good looking, it's impossible not to get noticed. I'll try not to be the center of attention but no promises."

That broke the tension for Eve and Jack.

"Just because you can't recognize greatness, doesn't mean everyone else is blind," Tex added.

A few minutes later, they turned on a road that had water on both sides. Water came up to the wall the road was built along, and there was a port visible in the distance. On the other side was a beach, and children were playing in the water next to others who were bathing or doing laundry. Children were children, no matter the circumstances or location. If they were given a chance to be kids, they would play and enjoy the innocence that they all have—until the world takes it away from them. She couldn't suppress the smile at watching them play in the water. There may still be hope for this place.

They drove to a massive and luxurious building on its own peninsula, standing out from its surroundings. Pulling up to a small checkpoint with a guard, the driver stopped and spoke in French. The guard recognized the hotel's driver but still went through the motions of checking his identification. He scanned the vehicle's interior through the open window and nodded when he saw the well-dressed Westerners in the back. He waved to the second guard in the shack, and the security arm raised to allow them to enter Kempinski hotel's parking area.

While nothing spectacular, the parking lot was still distinctly different from everything else they had seen so far. It was set up like any major hotel chain parking lot would be. It was clean and had plenty of well-tended plants to give it a welcoming appearance. They could have easily been anywhere else in the world. It wasn't until they got out of the vehicle that the smell and the heat reminded them exactly where they were. Bellhops were waiting to take care of their luggage, and Elle left them to it without a second glance. Everyone followed her lead, but Jack lingered a moment, seemingly uncomfortable with leaving his bags in the hands of strangers.

"It's fine, Jack. If they break it, they will replace it and pay more for the inconvenience." Elle made her voice lend an air of boredom to her words, but she held Jack's eyes to make sure he remembered who they were supposed to be.

Straightening, Jack replied, "I suppose the right price could make up for the irritation." He didn't sound convinced, but the words and his change in demeanor were enough to satisfy Elle that he would play his part. He fell in behind them as they walked into the hotel proper.

The change in their surroundings was jarring. The air was cool, clean, fragrant, and the entire area was opulent. Shiny marble floors, vaulted ceilings with chandeliers, and gold-framed artwork fit for a palace lined the walls. The hotel would have been beautiful in any context, but after the extreme poverty they had just seen, it seemed unreal. The disparity made it feel like they had entered another world entirely.

Elle braced for the change, remained stoic, and took the lead. Her confident, determined stride combined with the red suit made it impossible for anyone to look away. With all eyes on her, Tex was able to take a moment to subtly remind their less experienced companions to control their expressions. Walking straight up to the hotel staff, Elle focused in on the manager before the man could even introduce himself. The cut of his suit, and the slight deference the others showed the man, might as well have been a beacon.

"I trust our suite is ready," Elle stated.

The man was taken aback for only a brief moment before his practiced smile returned, and he replied, "Yes, Mademoiselle Alexander. I am Monsieur Pellau, the hotel manager, and I will take you there now. Unless you would prefer to dine first? Or enjoy a cocktail?"

"Perhaps later. For now, we would like to rest from our travels." Elle paused briefly before adding, "As long as everything is to our liking." Elle did not miss the flicker of unease in his expression. This man was on someone's payroll, and she would bet he had bugged their room. The question was, who was his employer? The government? Number 7? Another player? She needed to tread carefully until she figured out which puppet master was pulling the strings.

Keeping the smile plastered on his face, Pellau said, "We will make certain that you have everything you need, mademoiselle. If anything is not to your liking, we will see it changed immediately. Please, do not hesitate to ask."

Elle smiled. "I hope so, monsieur."

The man gave a slight bow and directed them to their destination with a sweeping motion of his arm.

Elle turned and nodded to her team, and they fell in behind her as they followed Pellau to the elevators. They watched as the bellhops disappeared into a service elevator with their luggage. Elle assumed they were going through the bags while en route to the room. There was a note of tension in Pellau's face as he followed her gaze. Elle was making him nervous, and he was likely rethinking the orders he'd given. *Good.*

Inside the elevator, Pellau seemed to debate how to proceed before returning to his typical routine. "Have you stayed with us before?" He asked the team, careful not to meet Elle's eye.

Tex didn't miss a beat. "Shouldn't you know that already?"

Pellau's smile faltered slightly. He was definitely worried now. "My apologies if I offended you, monsieur. I only meant for polite conversation. Our registries did not have your names listed, but it is always best to ask."

"I was expecting a delivery," Elle said.

"The couriers arrived this morning, mademoiselle, and your delivery was placed in your suite as instructed."

The elevator arrived at their floor. Pellau exited and held the doors for them. The floor only had two suites on it, and he led them to the one on the northern side. Using a key card, he opened the doors with a flourish before stepping out of the way. Elle walked in, and although she was impressed with the accommodations, she did not react. They walked through a short entryway into an open room with high ceilings. The far wall was comprised of a massive picture window that showcased a beautiful view of the water. The furnishings were white and gold, and the marble floors were accented with oriental rugs. Sitting on the floor next to the dining table were two duffle bags. *Game on.*

Turning back toward the door as their luggage arrived, Elle watched Pellau. He was studying the bags to see if he could detect anything amiss. His eyes tracked them as they were placed in the room. When he turned to speak, he was startled to see her watching him. "Would you like a tour of your suite? I'd be happy to point out all of the complimentary amenities."

"That won't be necessary," Elle replied levelly.

"Of course. We will leave you to get settled in and relax. "Show us where you would like your luggage to be placed, and we will happily move them to the correct rooms for you." Addressing Elle directly, he said, "Where would you like your bags, mademoiselle?"

"Right there is fine."

Pellau swallowed visibly but renewed his smile. Addressing the team, he asked, "Is everything to your liking so far?" Then, he surveyed the room as if to ensure that it was correctly set up.

Elle watched him closely. His gaze seemed to linger for a fraction of a second on the entertainment center and then shot up to the ceiling before coming back to the bags.

"I was hoping for a more modern décor, but this will do," Eve said as she walked over to the window and sat down on the chaise. She didn't even bother to look at the man she was talking to, coming across every bit like royalty addressing a servant.

Elle was impressed that Eve could act out of character so convincingly. The woman had hidden talents.

Jack made a grumbling sound in the back of his throat that suggested he was less than impressed and joined Eve by the window. Red Shirt went to the bar, and Julian leaned casually on the couch behind Elle, watching Pellau.

"If you would prefer to switch rooms, we have another suite that has a different color palette with a more modern aesthetic." Pellau sounded a little too willing to be accommodating. He wanted them out of this room, which told Elle he was afraid that she saw through him. He was right.

"This will do. We'll call if we need anything further," Elle said.

Tex moved to the door, signaling it was time for them to leave.

Inclining his head, Pellau took a breath and followed the bellhops out. Once he was gone, Elle turned to Jack. "Make sure none of your things were damaged in transit. I would check everything to make sure there isn't even so much as a scratch on it." Elle suspected that their luggage had been electronically tagged in the elevator, which meant that his gear might be compromised.

Jack grimaced. "If I find a single scratch, I'll make them pay up big time. My equipment is top of the line."

"Julian, why don't you turn on some music or find a movie on the TV?"

Julian glanced at the entertainment center and then back at Elle as he moved to it, eyebrows raised in question.

"You might have to search for a while, but I'm certain there must be something that will catch your interest."

Julian looked at the entertainment center appraisingly, trying to figure out where to start looking for hidden devices.

Looking at Tex, Elle said, "There's so much natural light in here. Why in the world would they leave the floodlights on? It makes things look a little yellow, don't you think?"

"I was wondering about that. I thought it was just me. I think the light switch is over here." Tex flipped off the lights, and the room dimmed slightly. It was almost midday outside, and the sun provided more than enough light. Moving with Elle to the center of the room, Tex followed her eyes to the ceiling and said, "I wonder what kind of crap they use for bulbs around here. Bet it's some cheap shit."

"I'll take that bet. Give me a boost?"

Elle climbed up onto Tex's shoulders and balanced carefully as she reached for the light fixture. There was some heat coming off the bulb, but not enough to burn her skin. It hadn't been on long. She twisted the bulb until it pulled free from the socket and saw what she was looking for—a small camera housed in the side of the fixture. It was angled to cover the room and inset so that even someone looking directly into the fixture would struggle to see it. If the light had been on, it would have been perfectly camouflaged and impossible to find.

Pulling the camera out of the housing to angle it directly at her face, she glared into the lens and said, "This is your only warning. Tell whoever holds your leash that these amateur tricks are only going to try my patience. Leave us to our business, and I will allow this little irritation to pass. Try anything else, and I promise you will regret it." Then, she ripped the camera from the housing, cutting its power.

CHAPTER 8

They found a total of two cameras, six GPS trackers, and six audio transmitters. The second camera had been inside the stereo speakers, and they each had found a tracker hidden in their clothes. Jack's equipment had been tampered with, but they hadn't been able to crack his defenses in the time they had. His gear was clean, but that didn't stop him from fuming about having someone mess with his toys. Within an hour, Jack had cleared all the rooms and destroyed the devices. Still irritated by the attempt on his laptop, he went back for a second round to make sure he hadn't missed anything.

Each bedroom and the kitchen had an audio transmitter. Between those and the cameras, there would have been nearly full coverage of the suite. The GPS trackers were for individual movements. The more they found, the less likely it became that the surveillance was from any government entity. While she wouldn't put something like this past Russia or China, it just didn't fit with their current situation. There would be no reason for those governments to look at them here unless their covers had been blown, and DJ wouldn't put in that much effort. That left her quarry as the most likely one responsible. It made the most sense, given the location and circumstances. But why? She knew they would face scrutiny, but this seemed excessive. Had they tripped an alarm with 7?

Elle pondered that possibility as they pulled out the weapons and ammunition in the duffle bags, inspected each piece, and did function checks. They were perfect. "Let's get these ready to go and stowed. Then, finish unpacking and get some rest."

"What time do you want to get started tonight?" Tex asked.

"Let's call it 2130."

Tex let out a sigh. "You know, Mama, we really need to talk about the way you treat us. Making me stay in a place like this, giving me toys to play with, and then forcing me to go drink at the Sky Bar in between hunting bad guys...we should probably get hazard pay for this."

"Well, princess, I suppose you're just going to have to suck it up and deal." Looking at Julian and Red Shirt, she asked, "Who's on watch tonight?"

"I am," Julian said.

Shit. "Fine, Robert, you're up. I hope you've been paying attention. They have a boutique shop in the hotel that has suits and onsite tailoring. Go get something appropriate to wear and charge it to the room." Elle could barely tolerate the arrogant smile on his face or the gloating look he shot Julian, but she kept going.

"Everyone get settled and get some sleep. We need to be at our best tonight. Eve, feel free to go all-out getting ready. Go for stunning. I want you turning heads. Tonight is about getting noticed. That's why we're only leaving one of us behind. Jack, Eve will help you get ready, so you can stop looking like you're going to be sick. You won't need to do much except have a good time. I know talking to people is not your forte, but that should work to our advantage. Keep conversation to a minimum. With the right attitude, you could pull off an air of mystery that will make every woman in the room pay attention."

Jack blushed and shifted his weight nervously.

Tex smiled at him. "Hey, man, you did great playing the part with the bags. You've got this. If you get into trouble, I've got you."

"And I'll help make sure you look the part," Eve added.

"Don't worry, Jack, you can still wear your Superman briefs if it helps you feel more like Clark Kent," Elle said.

"Very funny, Elle."

Tex, Julian, Robert, and Elle cleaned and reassembled the weapons and hid them in their rooms. Once that was done, they ordered room service and finished unpacking. When their food arrived, Elle asked for one of the dish covers. The server looked confused but handed it to her regardless. Moving back to the kitchen, she took all the destroyed devices they had found and placed them neatly on a plate. Taking a piece of the hotel's stationery, she wrote a short note: *Pellau, consider this a reminder between friends. Make sure we stay that way.*

Smiling, Elle placed the cover on the dish with the note on top and returned it to the room service cart. "Please make sure that Monsieur Pellau receives this directly."

The man bowed his head and left the room.

By the time Pellau received the message, the contents would be spreading like wildfire throughout the staff. The bold move would keep them guessing whether she was a potential friend or an enemy. That would buy her some freedom of movement.

After the meal, Elle finished unpacking and spent some time selecting what she would wear that night. Setting the alarm for 2000, she settled into the bed to get some sleep.

• • •

Elle's alarm interrupted a nightmare, causing her to bolt upright in bed. She was covered in sweat. Shutting the alarm off, she sat on the side of the bed for a while to let her heart rate settle back into a normal rhythm. Anger and frustration warred with each other inside her mind. The emotions made her want action, she needed…something. Anything to channel what she was feeling. Getting to her feet, Elle plugged her new iPod into the room's speaker system and scrolled through the playlists to hard rock. Hitting shuffle, the first song that came on was AC/DC's "Thunderstruck." *Yes.*

Elle showered and dried her hair, letting the music keep her pumped up for what was to come. Dressing in black lace underwear and a pushup bra, she added a garter belt with three throwing knives around her right thigh before pulling on her dress. The dress had a deep V-neck that showed off her cleavage and hugged her body, flaring at the hips. The material gathered around her hips in a way that didn't cause it to add inches but fell loose enough that it flowed when she walked and allowed her to wear a holster—or, in this case, knives—discreetly underneath.

Returning to the bathroom mirror, she took in her reflection. She put on diamond earrings and a sleek diamond and platinum necklace that nestled perfectly between her breasts. By the time she finished applying her makeup, she felt dangerous and unstoppable. Leaving her hair down and a little wild, she put on her heels and put her room key, cell phone, and money into a small black handbag. Looking around, she made sure that nothing of value was left easily exposed in case they had any visitors in their absence. Satisfied, she took one last look at herself in the mirror. She was ready.

Leaving her room, Elle met the team in the living room.

Jaws dropped when they saw her, particularly Julian's, but Elle gave him a look, and he regained a professional demeanor.

"You look amazing, Elle," Eve gushed. She was absolutely gorgeous in a green cocktail dress that looked like it had been tailor-made for her body.

"I suppose you clean up alright, Mama," Tex's roguish good looks were set off to perfection in a black suit and shirt that was open at the neck with no tie.

The big surprise was Jack. He could have walked off the pages of *GQ* with his gray suit and perfectly styled hair. Elle whistled a catcall at Jack and couldn't suppress the smile when he squirmed. "Well done, Eve. Jack, you look all grown up."

"I know. Can you believe it?" Eve added, smiling brightly.

"I feel ridiculous. Eve spent like ten minutes putting some crap in my hair and keeps yelling at me when I try to touch it," Jack said.

"It looks great, Jack. Don't mess with it," Eve said, looking like a proud mom.

"You put enough product in it that it should survive an F5 tornado. I don't think me touching it will make a difference. It feels weird." He started to raise his hand to touch his head, but Eve snatched it before he could.

Checking the time, Elle said, "Everyone ready to do this?"

"Do you really need to ask?" Tex stood and buttoned a single button on his jacket, and Eve and Jack nodded and took deep breaths to steady their nerves.

"Now this is my idea of a special mission," Red Shirt said as he entered the room.

Elle tried not to roll her eyes. He was wearing a suit with a slender, modern silhouette. It was tailored perfectly, but the cut made his movements appear stiff. He'd probably rip every seam if he moved too fast.

"Jack, are you all set in here?" Julian asked.

Nodding, Jack pointed to the laptop that was set up on the dining room table. "Once we leave, I'll activate it, but I set up a program to monitor for any movement. It's focused on the door, so if anyone comes in, the motion will turn the camera on and send us a text message. I'll be able to pull up a video feed from my phone, so we can see what's going on in real time. And Julian will have an extra set of 'eyes' on access points. I've also got sensors on the vents and windows just as an extra precaution in case someone goes James Bond on us."

The laptop looked completely normal sitting on the table. Anyone who came in would likely go right for it, giving them perfect footage of the intruder. "Do you have it set up to record?" Elle asked.

"Yes, we'll be able to review video whenever you want."

"Good job. I don't think our surveillance will try anything this soon, so we should be clear for tonight, but eventually, they'll make a move. If they come tonight, Julian, I need you to handle it. Play mind games—anyone who comes at this point will just be your average lackey. I would say barely veiled threats should do the trick. Leave them off-balance and scared. Call Tex if anything feels off or you need backup.

"If they interrupt my time with the ladies, they will definitely leave off-balance and scared," Tex replied.

"Alright, let's do this." Elle turned to the door, and her team followed her out into the hall and into the elevator. Pushing the button for the top floor, Elle felt the thrill of the chase. Every nerve ending was charged and ready for anything. She felt electric.

They reached the floor and exited the elevator into a short hall with black, glass doors at the end. The bass from the music made the floor beneath them pulsate. Without hesitation, Elle pushed open the door and walked into the Sky Bar like she owned it. There was a purple tint to the lighting that gave the area a night club feel. The place was decadent. The view outside the floor-to-ceiling window opposite the entrance was spectacular, with lights from the port and several boats sparkling on the dark water.

The layout of the bar was for socializing. Lush couches and chairs were set in groups for comfort while catering to the clientele's desire to see and be seen. In a country where money and power walked hand in hand, those with money wanted to be seen. This was the place to be in Djibouti City for that. If you were a power player in this area, you came here regularly to solidify your position. It spoke volumes that her target made this his regular haunt. He had cultivated a small empire here, and he was making sure that everyone knew who was actually in charge.

Scanning the area as she approached the bar, she took in the layout and was not at all surprised to see that their entrance had caused a stir. It was a busy night, and the bar was almost full. Everyone was beautifully dressed, whether they were there for business or pleasure. Even the escorts were high-priced in the Sky Bar. Men stared openly at Elle and Eve, and the women sized up Tex, Jack, and Red Shirt. It would only be a matter of time before women were hanging on them.

Elle felt eyes on her, but instead of being repulsed, it invigorated her. She needed to draw all the attention, to be the most desirable woman in the club. Her target needed to take notice. The crowds parted for them as they approached the bar, and she claimed a spot in the center. Ordering a bottle of Dom Perignon, Elle continued to survey the crowd. She was not a fan of the expensive champagne, but she wasn't drinking it for pleasure. They needed to showcase an image of wealth and success.

As the bartender moved to get the champagne, she saw a large alcove that served as a VIP area. It was perfectly placed to give the occupants a singular view of the establishment's main floor and the water. Inside, there were several men but twice as many women. All of them were watching Elle and her team. In the center, with a woman on either side of him, was her target. Number 7 was a handsome man with blond hair, a muscular physique, and an air of danger about him. It wasn't surprising that several women were vying for his attention, but right now, all of his attention was on Elle.

Elle had no doubt that he had already pulled everything he could find on their aliases and received reports from her interactions from Pellau. Now, he was sizing them up. She met his gaze with confidence and an aura of danger all her own. He smiled a cocky grin and raised his glass. She allowed a knowing smile to appear on her face before she inclined her head slightly and then turned her attention back to her team. *Gotcha*.

For the next hour, she sat at the bar and socialized with anyone brave enough to approach. Men and women alike came up, all preening and expecting to have their wealth or position entice them. Her team played their roles flawlessly. Flirting but staying aloof, stringing every would-be suitor along and building interest. Red Shirt's flushed cheeks and slightly slurred speech told her was enjoying himself too much. For her part, Elle smoldered, every movement and gesture intentional. The impact it was having on every man who walked up to her was clear, but they were not who she was performing for. Elle didn't look at him, but she felt Number 7's eyes on her. She waited, biding her time for what she knew was coming.

Finally, one of the men who was with Number 7 walked up and offered his arm. "We would be delighted if you would join us in the VIP area."

Elle looked at the man and then back at Number 7, appearing to consider the offer. Number 7 was still sitting casually in his seat, but the women had moved. He had cleared a spot for her right next to him, assuming she would accept the offer. Turning back to the man, she smiled and said, "Thank you. I appreciate the offer, but I can find my own way…when I'm ready." She turned back to her team.

She knew when the man had moved away by watching Tex's eyes. He followed the movement, and Elle could tell that her unexpected response had the desired effect. Tex met her eyes and gave her a half-grin. He knew she had Number 7's full attention. The man could not help but be fascinated with her now, and likely aroused. But she needed to play this next part out carefully to avoid turning the fascination into frustration or worse, anger. Finishing her drink, Elle stood up, nodded to her team, and walked to the VIP area.

Number 7's eyes were trained on her, the smile on his face, predatory. As she was approaching, she noticed several men had moved to one side and appeared to be playing darts and making rowdy bets. When she got closer, she realized they were using knives, with marginal success. Elle sauntered up to the area and made a show of glancing at the dartboard with a mildly amused expression. Returning her gaze to 7, she intentionally looked down at her leg, knowing his eyes would follow hers. She raised the hem of her dress to expose the knives on her thigh and returned her eyes to 7. When she looked back at him, she saw he was ready to act. He may be a playboy, but he was still a fighter through and through.

She gave him a sultry smile then turned toward the board, drawing the knife and throwing it in one fluid motion. The blade flew between the men and landed in the center of the bullseye. The men jumped and turned around in shock. Two of them moved their hands under their jackets in reaction. *So, these men are armed, even here. Good to know.* Elle dropped the hem of her dress and kept moving as if nothing had happened.

She had 7's undivided attention now, and his eyes bore into her. Sitting next to him, she leaned in, intentionally giving him a generous view down the front of her dress, and took his drink, regally taking a sip. It was rum and coke. "Interesting friends you have," she said by way of greeting.

"I could say the same for you," he replied in heavily accented English.

Elle smiled enigmatically. "I like to keep things entertaining."

"Entertaining isn't the word I would choose for you, belle."

"What would you choose?"

"Deesse."

"Goddess? Not quite but thank you."

A smile broke out across his face, "You speak French? Just when I thought you could not be more perfect." Turning toward her, he put an arm around the back of her seat and leaned in. "What brings you here tonight, belle?"

"The promise of adventure."

"Business or pleasure?"

"Is there a difference?"

"Not in my world." He placed a hand on her knee and slowly started to run it up her thigh.

"You don't want to do that."

He paused. "Yes, I do." Moving his hand back to her knee with a smile, he added, "But since it may be the last thing I do in this world, I'll be patient. There are still other things I would like to experience first."

"Such as?"

He gave her a speculative look that turned devious. "You said you were looking for adventure?"

"Always."

Number 7 stood and offered her his hand. "Then come with me, belle."

Elle hesitated before she took his hand and allowed him to pull her up. She was relishing this role and the thrill of the game. She felt so alive and sexy; it was a heady combination. The first moves in any op are risky, too many unknowns. In this world, one slip could have life and death consequences for all of them. She had to trust that Tex would look out for the others and that they would be okay without her. There was no turning back now.

Leaving the VIP area, Elle smiled at Tex when she caught his eye. His glance behind them told her the others were coming, too. She nodded and kept going.

In the hallway, 7 took her to a private elevator. Before they got on, one of the men handed him something, which he pocketed before she could identify it. When the doors opened, she expected everyone to enter, but 7 waved them off and told them to take the next one. As soon as the doors closed, he turned to her, his eyes hungry. He crowded into her space, expecting her to give ground. She didn't. Leaning in close, she thought he would kiss her, but he stopped at the last second. Reaching into his pocket, he pulled out the knife she had thrown at the board and showed it to her. "May I?" He breathed against her lips.

Lifting the hem of her dress and moving her leg to expose the empty sheath, she said, "Since you asked so nicely."

Keeping very close but not touching, he turned his head to look down the length of her body. He slowly seeded the knife back into place, his fingers grazing her skin and creating little pangs of desire. The erotic pull of the moment was almost too much to resist, but she couldn't be the one to yield. The mission depended on her ability to stay in control. Deciding to fight fire with fire, she took a deep breath, knowing it would move her breasts to within a fraction of an inch away from his lips and made a soft moan of satisfaction in the back of her throat. "Thank you," she said. And continued to hold her ground when he finally straightened back up. Her lips were a hairsbreadth away from his, and her eyes challenged him to resist.

Smiling, he said, "What's your name, belle?"

"Elle."

"Gerard. And this has been an unexpected pleasure, Elle."

"Does that mean the night is over already?"

"Oh no, it's just begun." Taking her hand as the elevator came to a stop, 7 led her out onto a beautiful, stone patio that surrounded an infinity pool. It was lit up with soft, blue lights, and there were cabanas set up around the outer edge. They continued through the area to a private pier with a sleek, black speed boat moored to it. Climbing onboard, 7 opened a compartment and pulled out two glasses and a bottle of rum. He mixed a pair of drinks, and then handed one of them to Elle before settling down beside her. Pointing to one of the boats in the distance, he said, "That one is mine. Once my friends get here, we will head out."

"A nighttime cruise in the Gulf of Aden?" Elle asked.

"What better way to hunt for pirates?"

CHAPTER 9

Number 7 watched closely for a reaction. *He's testing me.* Elle gave a mischievous smile. "I'm afraid I didn't accessorize very well for a night like that. But I suppose I can make do."

Movement by the pool caught their attention, and they turned to see 7's men coming out of the hotel with several women still hanging on their arms. When they reached the cabanas, the women broke off with some lingering kisses and fondling. After the women settled in to wait poolside, the men moved to the pier. There were five of them. And based on their reactions to seeing her in the boat with 7, this was typically a men-only event.

Good.

Eyeing her curiously, the men boarded the boat, and within minutes, they were speeding across the black surface while a white spray of water kicked up high in their wake. Elle closed her eyes and enjoyed the feel of the wind and the salt air.

Besides being shark-infested, the waters around the Horn of Africa were heavily populated by pirates and smugglers. It was the wild west. The only place that was probably worse than the Gulf of Aden was a little further to the east off Somalia's coast. Weapons, drugs, people—it didn't matter; it all was smuggled in these waters, making them extremely dangerous. Everyone was a potential target for attack from pirates, and smugglers were known to defend their cargo violently.

Instinctually, she knew she was being watched. Opening her eyes, she looked directly into 7's gaze without surprise.

"I thought I knew every beautiful woman who could handle a blade."

"Bet you say that to all the girls," Elle said with a smile.

"Do you have business here?" he asked.

"Don't we all? Why else come to a place like this?"

"What is your business?"

"Consider me a professional adventure seeker."

He laughed. "Aren't you going to ask any questions about this adventure?" he asked.

"What questions do you think I should be asking?"

"Don't you have any interest in where we're going or what is going to happen?"

"You said we were going pirate hunting. We're in the Gulf of Aden, so there is a fairly dense population of them. Since you have that beautiful yacht over there, I imagine you'll bait them into an attack. Or, since its dark-colored, you may choose to run it in blackout conditions to close in on a specific vessel without detection. One way or the other, unless you have crew-served weapons on your toy over there, there will be hand-to-hand involved. Whether they board you or we board them, it's going to come down to close-quarter combat. If it were me, I would choose to board them. There's a risk of booby traps, and they'll have home-field advantage, but that could be mitigated by the element of surprise. After, you won't have to worry about the clean up on your yacht. You can just sink their boat and let the sharks take care of the mess."

"So, you think there will be killing involved?"

"You don't strike me as a catch and release kind of man."

Before she could blink, his hand closed around the back of her neck, and he pulled her in. The kiss was hot and demanding and sent her blood racing. Elle deepened the kiss and ran her hand over his chest to the center for leverage. Once it was in place, she broke off from the kiss and pushed him back. He moved with apparent reluctance, pausing to meet her eyes. The lust there was plain.

"You're lucky you're a good kisser; otherwise, that might not have gone so well for you. But if you keep it up, we may not make the hunt," Elle said.

"I'm starting to think that it may be worth missing…but, then again, I did promise you an adventure."

Pulling away, but keeping her close, Number 7 settled back in beside her. Looking ahead, Elle saw that they were almost to the yacht. It was gunmetal gray with black accents and appeared to be brand new. The vessel was sleek and luxurious and gave off the impression of power. As they pulled alongside, Elle could not help but admire the artistry behind its design. At the rear, there was an area to dock the speedboat. Two additional men were waiting for them as they arrived. Catching the mooring lines, the men secured the boat.

Number 7 exited first and offered his hand. Elle allowed him to help her onto the yacht and was not surprised when he held onto her hand. As he led her through the vessel, Elle took in every detail that she could. The yacht was a newer model and likely custom made. The doors leading to the docking area were re-enforced, and she could swear there was a Kevlar lining on them. The passageways were well lit, and the deck had a dark-gray, no-slip coating. They passed an engine room and what was likely fuel tanks and went upstairs to come out on the aft deck.

The deck was a large open space with dark, wood flooring, and light-gray, upholstered furniture. Elle could easily see this being a prime area for entertaining. At the end of the deck, a darkly tinted, sliding glass door led into the rest of the superstructure. Following 7 through the door, they entered a bar area complete with big-screen TVs and a pool table. It was extravagant, a rich man's playroom. Moving toward the bow, they went up another set of stairs through a string of guest rooms. The crew probably stayed on one of the lower levels in an area she had not seen yet. There was another heavily armored door before entering the bridge, and then they were in the main control area.

As soon as they entered, an older man stood up from the Captain's chair. He appeared to be in his sixties but still looked tough as nails. "The ship is ready as requested, sir. What are your orders?" the Captain asked.

Without a response, 7 walked over to the navigation computer and input coordinates. Turning back, he said, "People are trespassing in my territory, Marcel, interfering with my business, stealing my property, killing my men. And not once, but twice. We're looking for an old tanker called the *Black Eagle*. She'll have at least two speedboats tethered to her. You have the coordinates for their last known position. I want us running dark and silent. Bring me in as close as you can." With a smile, he looked at Elle and added, "We're boarding tonight."

This isn't just a test. It's an audition. For what?

Marcel seemed unsettled by Elle's presence, but he didn't say anything. He just nodded to 7 and turned to the helm.

The engines purred to life, and then they were moving.

Number 7 pulled Elle out of the control room and into the first room outside of it. It had a conference table with chairs, several monitors, and a closet that housed a small but well-stocked armory. Walking over to the open door, Elle started surveying the contents. She needed to approach this like she did every mission. If she was boarding a hostile vessel, she was going in prepared.

Habit took over as she focused on the task at hand. Selecting a short barrel MP-5 submachine gun, she began inspecting the weapon and conducting a function check. Satisfied that the gun was in excellent condition, she added a suppressor. Turning back to Number 7, she asked, "Do any of your guys have small feet?"

He was sitting at the table where he could watch her. His expression had been a mix of entertainment and admiration, but now he looked confused. "Why do you ask?"

"Well, unless the *Black Eagle* has a dress code, heels are a little much for an assault, don't you think?"

Laughing, he said, "I can honestly say the thought had never crossed my mind until this moment." Shifting to kick his feet up on the table, he said, "So you want to come with us?"

"Isn't that why I'm here?"

"You could watch from the bridge."

"What kind of adventure would that be?"

A wide grin spread across his face. "What kind indeed?"

Elle got the feeling he wasn't just talking about adventures anymore.

"Is there anything else you need, belle?"

"Mag pouches, an ammo belt or Molle vest, and a sling."

"Where did you learn how to handle weapons?" he asked.

"Girl Scouts. We can waste time going through the rest of my resume, or we can get down to business, and I can show you what I can do."

Kicking his feet off the table, Number 7 stood in one fluid motion and moved to her. He drew her closer and kissed her passionately. The heat between them was building when they both heard voices approaching. Breaking away, Number 7 drew her toward the table and pulled out a chair. Sitting down next to her, he held her gaze as his men entered the room. She barely noticed the looks they each gave her as they came in and sat around the table. The look on Number 7's face was sending tremors through her, a promise of things to come.

She turned away and chastised herself. What the hell was wrong with her? He was the target, and she had a job to do. *Focus, damnit.* Looking around the table, she counted six men. They were all large, in their thirties. Professional mercenaries, every one of them. Four seemed to think that her presence was some kind of joke, but two of them scowled openly. She was certain there had been many other women on this boat, just not while they were working. She would have her work cut out for her trying to win them over.

"Who's the Sheila?" Asked the blond across from her with a heavy Australian accent that was thick with arrogance.

"Drake, gentlemen, this is Elle. She's coming with us tonight."

Silence met 7's statement, and then someone snorted. "You're kidding, right?"

"I'm not, Max." *He must be the newest member of the team. British, unseasoned.*

The man at the other end of the table, the biggest scowler, asked. "Where do you want her, Gerard?" *He's Second-in-command, also French, disciplined.*

"Elle's with me tonight, Chase. I can handle things for both of us if necessary." Elle heard the meaning behind those words loud and clear. If she didn't perform well, she was dead.

The room was silent after that. It was apparent none of the men liked the idea but weren't going to question him. Elle surveyed the men, looking each in the eye directly. Drake tried to stare her down, so she held his gaze the longest.

"We should be reaching the coordinates within the next sixty minutes. Get ready. Sean, get Elle geared up. Let's move."

With that, the men left.

7 stood and offered his hand. Elle took it and allowed him to escort her across the passageway. Passing through another door, they came into the main cabin area—7's private quarters. The room was luxurious but masculine. He opened a closet door and pulled out a black shirt and pants, placed them on the bed, and then went back to looking through the closet. After a brief search, he turned to her and said, "I'm afraid I don't have anything close to your size. It will be bulky, but would you like a shirt to cover your dress?"

"I don't care what happens to the dress. I'll just buy another."

Elle sat down in a chair and watched 7. The predatory smile was there again, but he didn't approach her. Instead, he began to undress. Each move was fluid and decisive, and he held her eyes with his, watching her reaction. She schooled her features, but her heart was racing. As his shirt came off, she saw chiseled muscles and several scars. *Knife?* Unable to fight the flush that came to her cheeks as he unbuttoned his pants, she relaxed into it. Number 7 was commando, standing naked in front of her. He was incredible.

He started to pull on the clothes that he had selected from the closet. He had just buttoned his pants when there was a knock at the door. He called out for them to come in.

The man, who she remembered as Sean, came in with an armful of items and set them on the bar. Pulling the boots and socks from the pile, he handed them to her and said, "These are the best I could do. They're a man's size nine, and I got you some socks. You can layer if needed." *Another French guy, probably their logistics man. Seems almost bored. Didn't become a merc to be the supply guy.*

"Good thinking. Thanks." Since she wore a men's size eight, she could make this work. Kicking off her heels, she pulled on the socks and boots. Once they were laced, she went to the bar to see what else he brought. A rifle sling, an assortment of magazine pouches, gloves and a black Molle tactical vest. All the items were in excellent condition and top of the line. She started placing the pouches she needed in her preferred spots. She could feel both men watching her but didn't care. In fact, she welcomed the distraction of having Sean there. It gave her time to regain control of the situation. Once the vest was situated, she removed a hair tie from her bag for a ponytail. Pulling on the vest and gloves, she turned to the men. "You ladies ready, or am I doing this on my own?"

Sean looked uncertain about how to respond.

7 laughed. "I wouldn't miss this for anything, belle."

CHAPTER 10

Once they were outside of territorial waters, Marcel turned off the external lights, and the crew covered all the windows. Elle had no doubt they turned off their transponders, too. It was illegal but standard practice for anyone conducting nefarious activities. Only the white of the water churning in their wake, reflecting the moonlight, gave any indication of their whereabouts. From a distance, that would be almost impossible to detect.

Elle was on the deck with the rest of the assault team, watching and waiting for any sign of their quarry, calm but alert. They arrived at the coordinates and were now in search mode.

A shimmer off to the east caught her eye. It was too close to the waterline for a star. To the team, she said, "Nine o'clock, I'm guessing about five miles out. Someone else is running dark."

7 used the yacht's internal comms and called for Marcel to slow. Then they all gathered on the port side of the deck and watched the horizon where Elle had indicated. For a long time, nothing moved, and Elle started to doubt what she had seen.

"There's nothing fucking there," Drake said, "Damn woman is just seeing ghosts—"

He barely got the last word out before the shimmer happened again.

This time they all saw it. There was no doubt; it was another boat. It had to be the *Black Eagle* waiting for her next victim.

7 called in the location to Marcel and told him to change course to intercept. The men grabbed their gear and moved to the speedboat. Elle followed.

Elle felt the excitement of the hunt kick in. Her senses heightened as blood rushed through her veins. *Stay focused.* She kept getting swept up in the moment. This wasn't her mission, but she needed to use it to her advantage. Nothing revealed true character and built bonds faster than a firefight. She gave a passing thought to the men she was about to kill. The idea of killing on a whim wasn't appealing. But it was a means to an end. They would no doubt do worse to her if given a chance.

That thought led to another. Could she take out 7 and blame it on the pirates? *No, that's a rookie move.* It wouldn't accomplish her overall mission and would likely get her killed by the others. She needed to destroy his link to the terrorist network in a way that no one could pick up and continue it after him. Not to mention, everyone with any connections in the country saw her leave with 7. If she came back without him, it would be game over.

Gritting her teeth, she took a deep breath and recommitted to her plan: infiltrate, gather information, destroy from within. Despite the mental reset, her body still thrummed, and she couldn't deny that she wanted this. Needed it.

The yacht turned and slowed further. 7 wanted to avoid alerting the pirates to their position, and the slower they moved, the less likely that would be. Several of the men donned night vision goggles as they got closer. She heard Chase say, "It fits the profile, Gerard. I see small boats tethered aft. We're approaching her starboard side."

"Just talk normal and drop the nautical shit," Drake growled.

One of the other men, Rhen, placed a hand on Drake's shoulder, and he shut up.

Impressive. Elle's gut screamed a warning to be cautious around Rhen but that he also might be useful. Rhen had a quiet authority around him, and he seemed to be the only one on the team that Drake appeared deferential to. He was calculating, observed everything, and was a man of action.

"Everyone, head below and get ready," 7 ordered.

Elle followed the men back to the docked speedboat. Chase took the controls, and 7 sat next to her. Once they all boarded, 7 gave a series of orders to Marcel and the crew. The men holding the mooring lines cast them off as the engines came alive. She felt the yacht stop and turn before the docking area opened to the night sky. The hunt was on.

As they moved out into the night, it took a minute for Elle's eyes to adjust. She had not wanted to wear NVGs to preserve her night vision. She left the long-range defense to the men who chose them and were armed for it. They would watch the deck of the target vessel to make sure they were not spotted and blown out of the water before they even arrived. Moving at a pace that kept their approach as silent as possible, and to minimize the amount of water they churned up, the minutes stretched out for an eternity. The anticipation was building for the fight to come. Elle embraced it and shut out all other thought. This is what she lived for, the thrill.

Approaching the stern of the *Black Eagle*, she saw the ladder they used to access their speedboats. *How convenient for them, and now, for us.* These pirates have obviously never considered that they could be pursued. Chase expertly maneuvered their boat between the others and pushed in as close as possible to the ladder. Max grabbed it and tethered a line to hold them in place. Nodding to the others once it was secure, he waited for the signal to board. 7 surveyed the team. They were all poised for action. Using a hand signal, he gave them the green light. Max and Sean went first, followed by Drake and Rhen. Luke went next; he would find a high point and provide overwatch and cover fire as needed. Chase was staying with the boat, so Elle and 7 brought up the rear.

As she was about to climb, she caught a smile on 7's face. When she gave him a puzzled look, he stepped close and ran a finger across her bare leg before tugging on the hem of her dress. She almost laughed out loud. Even as they were about to go into a gunfight, he was focused on her. Elle felt wild and sexy and reveled in it.

The boots were a little too big and made her feel less coordinated, but she didn't think it would impact her performance if she stayed focused. As she reached the top of the ladder, she eased herself over as quietly as possible and moved to the side to allow 7 to join.

The rest of the men were posted, providing security, and Luke was moving onto the top of the pilothouse. As soon as he was in position, they moved out. The pirate ship was old and in need of some attention, but it seemed to function well despite the neglect. The smell was terrible, though. It was as if the crew had ceased caring about hygiene or the ship's cleanliness—probably thought it made them seem more terrifying somehow. Or, more likely, they just didn't notice anymore. Most of these guys spent their time drunk or high when they weren't killing.

As they reached midship, they broke apart.

Max and Sean continued to search the deck before moving to the crew quarters. Drake and Rhen headed to the engine room and cargo hold. She posted up next to the pilothouse with Number 7.

Not hesitating for a second, Elle took the lead and moved to the door. The hinges were outside on the right, so she positioned herself on the left. Elle waited for 7 to get behind her. As soon as he was in position, he tapped her shoulder, and she flung it open. She flew into the room, staying to her right and firing. Of the three men inside, she took out two before 7 got off his first shot, taking the third man in the head.

7 was moving to the left around the room while she continued right. They quartered every inch in overlapping fields of fire to cover the entire space. It wasn't large, but there were bulky equipment panels and chairs that created blind spots. They had to be certain no one else was there.

The room was clear.

Shouts came from outside, and they returned to the door. Men were running up from below decks, and they could hear gunshots now. Since each man on the team had taken a suppressed weapon, that meant the pirates were returning fire.

Several pirates went down the moment they cleared the hatch, and Elle remembered that Luke was above them. Without further thought, she went through the door and joined the melee. She ran to the ladder well. It would create a fatal funnel for any man who tried to come up while she held the high ground. Entering, she could see dark-skinned men approaching, and she opened fire. Keeping to the side, ensured she could not be taken out by a lucky shot and started down.

The first level was crew quarters. The stench was even worse. Looking around the landing, she saw sprays of blood on the bulkheads and several bodies. The passageway was narrow, limiting maneuverability. She didn't like it. Catching movement in the low light, she saw Sean come out of one of the rooms, followed by Max. They seemed a little surprised to see her, but nodded and moved away, toward the far end of the passage. It was barely wide enough for them to walk down without having to turn sideways. A door opened behind them, and a blood-soaked man with a machete emerged, charging at them, screaming. Elle fired, nailing him in the back. He pitched forward and hit the deck hard. She found herself looking at a startled Max. Sean was frozen in mid-turn. Both looked at her a little stunned. Inclining her head to them, she turned without a word and saw 7 watching from the ladder well.

Walking past him, she continued down the ladder well. He followed. They were in a fight, and he was evaluating her every move. He could put a bullet in her head at any time. It made her skin crawl, knowing there was a threat directly behind her, but she also knew she couldn't stop. She felt alive.

The next level was the cargo hold. There were numerous green, wooden crates spread throughout—an arms shipment. The boxes had Cyrillic writing on them and appeared to be both weapons and ammunition worth at least several hundred thousand dollars.

The stacks of crates created odd angles and plenty of areas for people to hide.

Elle started to clear the area systematically. As she did, she came across Rhen and Drake standing over an open container talking in hushed tones. When she moved into their field of view, they both drew down on her. For a moment, it seemed as though they were going to shoot, even after recognizing her. Elle lowered her MP-5 and, after an uncomfortable pause, they lowered their weapons. Feeling his presence again, Elle wasn't surprised when 7 stepped around her and approached the men. Rhen looked at ease, but Drake stiffened a little.

"Are we done here?" 7 asked.

"Engine room is clear, minimal resistance down here. Just a few drunk pirates. Looks like they haven't met with their buyer yet. Can't imagine they would hold onto all this for personal use," Rhen reported.

"Probably felt badass holding onto it," Drake suggested.

Reaching into the open crate, 7 pulled out a grenade. "Looks like several are missing. We need to watch for booby traps."

"Are we offloading?"

"Just the .50 cals and sniper rifles. Everything else sinks with this piece of shit boat."

"You're kidding, right?" Drake asked.

Number 7 looked at Drake levelly. "I'm not. We don't have the time or the room to offload everything using the speedboat, and, if this place is rigged to blow already, I'm not bringing the yacht any closer. I couldn't care less about the loss of merchandise. Our inventory can handle it. It's the potential impact on my business that I can't allow. There are always guns to buy, but, if you lose your buyer's confidence, it's all over. Reputation is everything in this world." From 7's tone, this had been a topic of discussion on more than one occasion. His patience was wearing thin.

"We're on it, Gerard," Rhen interjected so Drake wouldn't open his mouth again.

The two men turned and moved away.

Elle's mind raced along with her heart rate. She was keyed up from the fight. More importantly, she figured out how she was going to take down 7 and his organization.

7 watched Rhen and Drake walk away for a moment before his attention returned to her. For a second, time

halted, and she wasn't certain what would happen next. Movement behind her drew 7's eyes, and she spun around instinctually to face the threat. It was Sean and Max. They raised their hands, and Elle relaxed.

Over the next thirty minutes, they searched to find the correct crates and get them to the speedboat. They moved efficiently, keeping the possibility of traps in mind, but the crates were heavy and awkward. They could use the ship's cargo elevator to get them to the main deck, but there was no easy way to move them onto the speedboat. It took muscle and coordination. Once they finished loading, they used the explosives still in the cargo hold to rig the ship to blow on command.

After that, the team piled back into the speedboat, and Chase maneuvered them back to the yacht.

On the return trip, Elle embraced the feeling of the wind and salt air on her skin once again. She was on an adrenaline high. Before she knew it, they were back at the yacht and docking. She felt a little disappointed that it was over. The men were all amped, ready to drink and get back to their women. This is what they all lived for—the rush.

Number 7 ordered Marcel to go back to the hotel. After they started moving, he detonated the pirate's boat.

The explosion was spectacular.

The men cheered and poured drinks to celebrate.

But 7 didn't stay. He grabbed Elle's arm and led her back through the yacht. She didn't fight him but felt anticipation coursing through her veins. She wasn't surprised when they arrived back at his cabin, and she walked past him into the room as he locked the door. When he turned around, Elle's breath caught. The intensity in his expression almost caused her to back away reflexively.

He moved to claim her without hesitation. It was like he couldn't hold back any longer. When he reached her, his lips clamped down over hers aggressively. He pushed her into the bulkhead, trapping her against it with his body. Reaching down to hook his hands behind her thighs, he lifted her up. Elle wrapped her legs around his waist and met his intensity with her own. Running his hands up past her knives to her lace underwear, he gripped the top in both hands and ripped the garment away. The thin material didn't have a chance against the raging firestorm.

He spun away from the wall and carried her to the bed. There was no thought, only sensation. After he threw her down, he opened his pants. They didn't stop to undress any further, couldn't if they tried. Elle wanted—needed this—as much as 7 did and allowed the moment to take her over.

Their fever for each other didn't abate when they reached the first climax. If anything, it intensified. Finally pulling off his tactical gear, 7 undressed completely and then started undressing Elle. Every new inch of exposed flesh got his full attention, and he was hard and ready again. He ravished her body, greedily. Elle forgot everything beyond the building sensations. Taking control, she pushed him off and mounted him. Whatever surprise he felt at the change in position was overtaken by a new surge of pleasure. His hands and lips roamed over her possessively. When they reached climax this time, Elle saw fireworks behind her eyes.

Somewhere in the back of her mind, she knew staying detached and in control was vital, but she wanted to do that again. She had no idea how much time had passed, but gradually, she became aware that the yacht was slowing. That realization snapped her back to the mission. Leaning forward, Elle gave 7 one last passionate kiss before dismounting him. Her body ached deliciously, but she tried to ignore it. Gathering her clothes, she got dressed as though nothing had happened. Number 7 sat on the bed, watching, his curiosity evident. A man like him probably wasn't used to a woman who didn't linger, but Elle was ready to leave without a care.

With a smile, he got up, dressed, and walked over, offering an arm. Without a word, Elle took it.

They returned to the main deck, where the rest of the team greeted 7 before eyeing her with a knowing smile.

Typical.

Max, conversely, lifted his glass to her. She'd saved his life, after all. Sean also inclined his head. Elle returned the acknowledgment and then looked to the horizon. She could see the lights of the Kempinski hotel approaching. They would be anchoring soon.

"Would you like a drink before we go?" 7 asked.

"Rum and Coke."

He walked to the bar as she made herself comfortable on one of the lounge seats on the deck. She took in a deep, relaxing breath, and that's when the hair on the back of her neck stood on end. She turned. Rhen was watching her, assessing. He didn't turn away, so she held his gaze. She raised an eyebrow, a silent question. He smiled and returned to talking with Luke and Drake.

Returning with drinks, Number 7 sat next to her. Elle found herself relishing the moment, even though she was literally surrounded by the enemy. *Maybe I should consider a yacht of my own someday?*

"Did you enjoy your evening?" 7 asked.

"I did, surprisingly."

"Surprisingly?"

"It's not every day that someone lives up to their promises. You promised me an adventure, and I wasn't disappointed. Overall, I would say this evening has been very…satisfying."

Laughing, he said, "I am a man of my word."

"I can appreciate that." With that, she turned back to the horizon. She knew that her causal air was confusing and capitalized on it.

"How much longer will you be in Djibouti?"

"Until I get bored or something else catches my interest. Whichever comes first."

Elle felt the weight of 7's eyes studying her.

"Would you join me for dinner this evening?"

"A business proposal?" She made it more of a statement than a question.

"Perhaps. You'll have to show up to find out, belle."

CHAPTER 11

When they arrived back at the hotel, Elle started to walk back to her room with 7 by her side. It was close to sunrise, but there were still plenty of shadows around them. Once they were out of earshot of his men, she asked, "What do you want from me?"

He seemed startled by the question. "Isn't it obvious?"

"We had a good time tonight, Gerard, but I'm not stupid. I know you did your research, and you know what we do. We found your cameras, and I know the staff here is on your payroll. I get it, this little game you've been playing with me tonight. It was fun, but by now, you've realized we're not the competition. So, you can go about your business and leave us to ours. We'll move on when our job is done. There's no need to draw this out."

He gave her a penetrating look, but she didn't flinch. "What makes you think I would have anything to do with what you found?"

Elle turned to walk away.

He grabbed her arm and pulled her around to face him.

Elle restrained herself from punching him, but he must have seen the intent. He smiled and then kissed her. She deepened the kiss before pushing him away.

"Such fire. Come to the penthouse tonight at eight, belle. We should talk more."

With that, he released her. She gave him a half-smile and walked away. He didn't stop her again. Elle kept in character all the way back to her room, knowing that 7's eyes would be following her. As soon as she was inside the suite, she put her back to the door and closed her eyes, just breathing for a moment.

"About damn time, Mama," Tex said.

Opening her eyes, she was not surprised to see Tex waiting up, still in his suit pants and shirt. "Eve and Jack?"

"We're here, Elle." Walking into the living room, she saw them sprawled on the furniture in their evening wear. It looked like both of them had fallen asleep at some point. Julian walked into the room with a cup of coffee, his face was unreadable, but his eyes scanned her.

Elle suddenly felt exposed and guilty. *I didn't make him any promises.*

"Any issues after I left?" she asked.

"Just one, but we handled it," Tex began. "We got pretty popular when everyone saw you leave with that guy. They figured getting close to us would also get them close to you and the target. At least two women are madly in love with Jack now, and half the men in the bar tried to get Eve alone. I felt more like a bodyguard. Didn't stop me from stealing a few hearts, though. Haven't lost my touch."

"What was the issue?" Elle asked.

Tex's face darkened. "Robert. He drank too much and got into a pushing contest with some guy. Took some doing to get him out of there, but we managed."

"I can stay on watch until Robert sobers up," Julian volunteered.

"No. We're all here now. The likelihood that anyone would hit us now is low, but we'll use Jack's security set up as an early warning system. Get some sleep, we'll need you sharp later. Robert's done."

"How did it go for you?" Eve asked, a tinge of worry in her voice as she looked at Elle.

Elle avoided looking at Julian. "Good. I've got an in, and I know how we're going to take them down."

Jack yawned. "So, what's next?"

Walking over to Jack, Elle made a show of touching his hair. "Wow, it didn't move at all. Did you use glue, Eve?"

Jack smacked her hand away, and Eve gave her a peeved look.

Elle chuckled. "Good job tonight. All of you. Go and get a few hours of sleep. We'll link back up at noon. We have work to do."

Returning to her room, Elle undressed and got into the shower. As she was washing off the sweat and smell of carbon, she realized that 7 hadn't remarked on any of her scars. Strangely, she hadn't thought about them herself while she had been with him. He had to have noticed. Did it buy her more credibility? Pondering that possibility, she threw on shorts and a t-shirt and lay down to rest. She thought it would take a while to fall asleep and began to clear her mind. It didn't.

When Elle's alarm went off, she jerked awake. Disoriented, it took her a moment to remember where she was and to turn off the alarm. She had slept undisturbed for the first time in months, no dreams. The initial shock faded and was replaced by a moment of wonder before her head took over. *Why now?* Trying to let go of that train of thought, Elle forced herself to think of the task at hand. Sleep was critical to keeping physically and mentally sharp; figuring out "why" could wait until the mission was over.

Getting dressed in slacks and a blouse, she twisted her hair up in a messy bun and added earrings and makeup for the daylight hours. She usually wouldn't go to the trouble, but she had a suspicion they would have a visitor before her dinner tonight.

Her team was awake, too, hanging out in the common areas. Jack and Eve were still in their pajamas, but Tex and Julian were sweating in their workout gear. They must have just returned from the gym. Red Shirt was trying to cover his hangover but was failing.

"Hey, Elle, want room service?" Jack asked.

"That's fine. Just be ready to sweep it and anywhere the server moves while he's here after they drop it off."

"Seriously?"

"Just a precaution. I think our message was received yesterday, and 7 should leave us alone, but I don't think he's the only one with people on the payroll here."

"They better not bug my breakfast. I'm starving. You don't stand between a growing boy and food," Tex said.

After they ordered, Elle sent them off to dress. She set the TV to a movie channel that was playing *The Expendables*. The movie seemed appropriate for the situation, but even better, the action would provide a sound buffer, shielding their conversations from anyone attempting to listen from outside the room.

When their food arrived, the server seemed a little nervous but didn't make any moves that indicated he would try something. After he left, Jack swept the food and the area. All clear. Once they were finished eating, it was time to work. Placing the dishes in the kitchen, they cleared the table and got down to business.

"Jack, I need you to break into agency files for operations in the Horn of Africa. I want you to locate and copy an existing file that we can change to make it read like the target is someone who is involved in arms deals based in Djibouti. Make sure the metadata shows that the file was created at least six months ago; the modified date will be today. Keep the file number close to the original. If anyone is monitoring the reports from this area, they'll think they overlooked it by mistake or that there was a clerical error.

"Eve, use whatever travel dates and locations you have for 7. Keep the details vague enough so that they don't single anyone out, but make sure they point in the direction of 7 and his team. Help Jack pick a file that is deep into the asset development stages and ready for recruitment. I want you to write in a meeting that talks about the source's boss making rash decisions, being risk-adverse, and wasting an opportunity to make more money. Use every bad habit that drives you crazy when you read these reports as a guide. You want it to be interesting and attention-grabbing without giving away anything of substance. Then, I want you to update the handler notes to say that the asset will be paid to monitor weapons proliferation and the Fior network."

"The Fior network?" Eve asked.

"Our make-believe handler's name for his pet project. Wouldn't be the first time that someone stumbled onto an asset that could give them something huge. We're just making it look like it happened. If 7 is as good as I think he is, he's got someone monitoring field agent messages for any mention of his operations. We're going to give him one."

"Won't that alert him that there's a problem?" Jack asked, confused.

"Yes, which is what I want."

Jack stilled looked confused, but he shrugged it off and started typing on his laptop.

"What's the plan for tonight?" Tex asked.

"I'm heading to the penthouse for dinner. You and Julian are going to case for a meeting location."

"What's the meeting for?"

"To help keep up the pretense that we are here for a job of our own. Make it look like we are preparing for a clandestine meeting, so bring your 'A' game. These guys are professionals, and they likely use locals for their leg work to keep from standing out. We need to know what tactics they use and how vigilant they are. Do any of your new admirers from last night have lucrative connections?"

Tex grinned widely. "Several actually, but I think what you're looking for would be the exiled Ethiopian princess. Her daddy was the last monarch of that country, and he died in exile."

"Think she'd accept a dinner invitation from you?"

Tex looked affronted. "Who wouldn't?"

Laughing, Elle replied, "That's the meet you're planning for then. The diversion should buy us a couple of days."

"We're on it. Anything else?" Tex asked.

"GPS trackers. Something small and easily concealed. They need to attach easily to a weapons crate."

"How many?" Julian asked.

"Get a dozen."

"Done. Too bad we didn't keep the ones we found here," Julian said.

Elle shrugged. "Too easily traced back to us, and they wouldn't have fit in with what I have in mind anyway. Besides, that would make things too easy for you."

Julian smiled.

"What about me?" Red Shirt asked.

"You're on security watch from here on out," Elle said.

"You've got to be kidding me."

"I'm not. You had your shot, and you blew it. I'm not giving you any more chances to jeopardize this mission."

Red Shirt stood, slamming his thighs against the table, "Who the fuck do you think you are?"

A knock at the door interrupted the commotion. The team stiffened, but Elle had been expecting this. Ignoring Red Shirt, she walked to the door. When she looked through the peephole, her breath caught in her throat: Number 7.

She had expected the hotel manager or one of 7's men, not the man himself. A little rattled, Elle turned back to her team and held up seven fingers and pointed to the door. They nodded.

Elle opened the door and smiled. "I expected one of your minions."

"And what did you expect to happen, belle?"

"Flowers and some calculated lure designed to entice me to dinner."

His smile was charming as he pulled a single long-stemmed red rose from behind his back. "Then, who am I to disappoint?" The rose had a silver key tied around the stem with a black ribbon.

"What's this?" she asked.

"Your next adventure. If you're up for it."

Elle knew what he would say, but she still asked, "And what will it be this time?"

His expression was devilish, and he crowded in close, his breath tickling her skin. "You'll have to show up for dinner to find out."

She couldn't control the way her body naturally warmed to him. "Well played."

"I'll take that as a yes." He said, then placed a kiss on her cheek before walking away.

Closing the door behind her, Elle noticed the odd looks from her team and ignored them. "Things are moving forward as planned."

Red Shirt moved toward her menacingly while addressing the group, "Seriously, did no one else see that, or are you just too scared to say anything? Your girl here is sleeping with the enemy."

"You have no idea what you're talking about. Back off," Elle warned.

"All that bullshit about me jeopardizing this mission, how about you? Is there anyone you aren't going to screw?"

Her first punch connected with his face before she even realized what she had done. Rage surged through her as she landed a second punch.

Red Shirt bellowed and lunged for her.

She moved to dodge his counterpunch, but in the close quarters, he was able to land a glancing blow.

Tex and Julian jumped between them, restrained Red Shirt before he could continue the attack.

"That's enough!" Julian shouted.

Red Shirt thrashed for a minute before relenting. "Fucking let go of me."

When they released him, he glared at each of them in turn. "You want to follow your little whore here, go ahead. She's going to fuck you all in the end. I'm done." With that, he stormed off, slamming the door behind him.

For a long time, it felt like they were all holding their breath.

"Are you okay?" Eve asked, worried.

Suddenly feeling defensive, Elle shot back, "Of course I'm okay. I'm doing my job, which is what we should all be doing. So, let's get back to it. Tex, get that bastard out of here on the first available flight." Elle turned to go back to her room, catching their looks of skepticism on the way. They were not convinced.

Back in her room, she rifled through her clothes to select an outfit for the evening, but couldn't settle on anything. Her mind kept playing through different scenarios for the upcoming dinner with Number 7, drifting in directions she did not want it to go. She felt antsy again. She needed to do…something. Grabbing her purse, she walked out of the room and then left the suite. She heard Tex call after her but didn't stop. They had their orders.

Taking the elevator down to the main floor, Elle headed toward the high-end boutique across the lobby. It was a small but opulent store that catered to wealthy clientele. Inside, there were cocktail dresses, gowns, and even a couple of high-end suits. Elle found herself drawn to a white pantsuit. Normally she avoided white but not today. She wanted to go bold.

CHAPTER 12

When Elle returned to the suite, she found Jack absorbed in his laptop and Eve taking notes on a legal pad while looking over his shoulder. She didn't see Tex or Julian. Eve looked like she wanted to say something, but Elle didn't give her a chance. Taking the purchases from the boutique to her room, she closed the door and began removing tags. A soft knock on the door did not surprise her, but the rush of irritation did.

Mentally chastising herself, she called out for Eve to enter.

"Are you angry at us, Elle?"

Damnit, I am. But why? Because they didn't like the way she was acting with 7? "I'm just annoyed. You all said you wanted to be part of this, and yet you question me at every turn."

"That's not fair, Elle. We're just concerned. You've been acting out of character ever since you came back. This is all new to us, and we're not sure what's going on. After everything that's happened, how could we help it?"

"I'm fine. You don't need to worry about me." As soon as the words were out, Elle inwardly cringed.

Eve wasn't buying it either. "Say it all you want. It doesn't mean we're just going to stop caring."

Elle sighed. "Let's just stay focused on the mission. I know you care, Eve, I really do. But I can't think about all this right now. I'm fine. What I really need more than anything is to keep going."

"If you don't take care of yourself, how do you expect to finish the mission?" She paused a moment before adding, "Is this really what you want, or do you think you have no choice?"

Frowning, Elle studied Eve's face. She was worried, but it was more than that. "What do you mean?"

"This mission has turned your life upside down in more ways than one. There's no denying it. And you'd have to be a fool or suicidal to not question whether all of this has been worth it. You're not either of those things, Elle, but you have a stubborn streak a mile wide. You have a right to do what's best for you, regardless of what others think. I just worry that you're too lost in all of this to really know what that is."

Words failed her for a while, and she just looked at Eve. She wanted to say something harsh, but true concern was written all over Eve's face. Elle knew that Eve was only thinking about her well-being and that making any cutting remarks would be petty. Sitting on the bed, she took several cleansing breaths and looked out the window. "It's true. These last several months have not been easy, and I'm still dealing with the fallout. But the one thing that has kept me going is the need to finish the mission. This work is all I have. It's who I am. I need it more now than I ever did before. It's the only thing that keeps me from losing my mind. Half the time I feel like I'm going to crawl out of my own skin if I don't do something. Anything."

"You have us, too, Elle. You're so much more than the job, and you need to know that."

"What are you trying to tell me?"

"That no matter what, you're not alone in this. And we're going to watch out for you even if you disagree. We see you struggling to get back to the way things were. That's never going to happen. You seem out of control at times, and I'm betting it's because you're trying to force things into a direction that you're comfortable with. We've changed, and we all need to adjust—you more than any of us. Don't push us away, Elle, we're not your enemy."

Elle felt a surge of emotions at once—anger and sadness with fear at the center of it all. There was nothing she could say to dispute what Eve had said. "Please go, Eve. I want to be alone."

Eve shut the door behind her, leaving Elle alone.

Tears burned in her eyes, and her chest constricted. What the hell was wrong with her? She was doing so well. Why was she back to this? *No, I'm not doing this again.* Last night she had felt so alive and free. She had slept soundly and had been back in total control this morning. She needed that again, and action seemed to be the key.

She wiped away the tears and got up. Her body was still recovering, and she hadn't been taking care of it over the last couple of days. So, she changed into workout clothes and went to the gym. Luckily, she was the only occupant in the facility when she entered, although she wasn't really alone. Making a note of the security cameras, Elle knew she would be watched the entire time. Stretching to warm up, she forced herself to focus on her body. Her muscles ached, but remembering why brought a smile to her face. Refusing to think about the ramifications of her involvement with her target, Elle lost herself in the music pumping through her headphones and her usual workout routine. Before she knew it, an hour had passed, and it was time to get ready for dinner.

Returning to the suite, she was surprised not to see her team. Noticing the light on Jack's laptop, she walked over to see the camera was activated. Her cell phone buzzed. It was Jack.

"We're out at the pool. I wanted to test my gear."

Elle smiled. "And?"

"There is a slightly longer delay than I thought, but I think I can tweak it a little more now that I have this as a test run."

"Glad to be of service. Is everyone with you?"

"Eve is. We've still got some work to do, so we'll be heading back up soon. Tex and Julian haven't gotten back yet."

It hadn't been very long, but she felt a little anxious that they were still gone. "The sun is brutal here, Jack, make sure you wear sunscreen. This close to the equator, you can fry in record time."

"Thanks, mom. I swear between you and Eve…" Jack's grumbling trailed off.

Elle could just imagine the look Eve was giving him. Hanging up, she went to get ready for her evening.

She knew the right clothing could really sell a persona. The suit she chose for the evening was expertly tailored. The jacket was hip length with a single button closure. Under the jacket, she wore a white lace bustier that accented her figure to perfection. She added a pearl choker for a feminine touch, and her hair was back in the messy bun with tendrils hanging around her face. There was a knife sheathed inside the sleeve of her jacket. She felt beautiful, powerful and ready for anything.

At precisely eight, Elle rang the bell outside of the penthouse. When 7 opened the door, she saw his eyes sweep over her possessively before he stepped back to invite her in. Without a word, he closed the door and crowded in close. Time stretched out as she held his gaze without flinching.

Smiling, he pulled back and said, "You're going to make this significantly harder for me than I thought."

"Make what harder?"

"Trying a little old-fashioned courting, when all I can think about is how badly I want you."

Elle's breath left her in a rush. Schooling her features, she raised an eyebrow and said, "Is this a business proposition or a date?"

"It's both, belle. As I said, I think you and I have much to discuss."

"Such as?"

"First, let's enjoy a nice meal and get to know each other a little more." He offered his arm, and they walked into a beautiful dining area with an amazing view of the water.

The table was already set with an array of dishes. Instead of being formal and sitting at the far ends of the table, the place settings were right next to each other on one end. It was an intimate set up, and Elle was a little put off by it but smiled politely when 7 pulled out her chair. This was dangerous territory, and she found herself wishing for another gunfight instead.

The conversation started out innocent enough, but as it progressed, Elle found herself revealing real details about herself, talking about the loss of her parents, and learning to take care of herself in the foster care system. He was just as open with her, or so it seemed. His childhood had not been a happy one, and she found herself drawn into his story. Still, she shocked herself with how much of her past she was exposing. Did it matter? He was going to be dead soon anyway. Her gut clenched at the thought. *Shit.*

Taking control of the conversation, she said, "That's enough of our sad stories for one night, don't you think?" Holding up the key he had given her, she smiled. "It's been a lovely dinner, Gerard, but don't think you've managed to distract me from this. You said you had another adventure?"

Laughing, he said, "I do, belle." Standing, he offered his hand and pulled her to her feet. "Are you ready?"

"I'm always ready."

As they were about to leave, his cell phone rang. He looked at the caller ID and answered it. "What's happening?" 7 gave her a speculative look as he listened.

Her pulse raced, as the look on 7's face was all business. Her intuition screamed that this call could only be about one thing: Red Shirt. *If that bastard burned me, I'll kill him.*

Gerard hung up. "It seems there is an issue with two of your people."

Elle's stomach lurched. "What?"

"The hotel staff knows to keep me informed of anything that happens on these grounds. One of your men, Robert, I believe is his name, has been drinking heavily by the pool for the last hour. The staff and other guests have been keeping their distance because he's been aggressive toward them. It wasn't concerning this late at night, since he was the only person out there. But, then, the other woman with you, Eve, approached him, and an altercation ensued. Robert has taken her inside the pool house, apparently against her will."

No!

Anger propelled Elle from the suite. Not wanting to wait for the elevator, she hit the stairs at full speed. She needed to focus, but all she could think of was getting to Eve. Elle didn't even want to think about what Red Shirt could do.

She burst through the door to the pool area and was outside the pool house moments later. Pausing at the door, she saw a very faint light coming from inside. Pulling a knife from the sheath up her sleeve, she tried the door and discovered it was locked. She didn't have time to return for her lock pick set, so she went with the only other option.

She pounded on the door. "I know you're in there, you little bitch. Your half-assed scheme is over. Why don't you stop hiding? Come out here so we can finish what we started. If you think you can."

The move was a blatant attempt to draw him out, and Elle had no doubt that he knew it. But it would kill his ego, and she needed that to override any thoughts of self-preservation. She kept heckling him, "I'm out here all alone, and you're too much of a fucking coward to face me. Too scared of a woman. Got your feelings hurt, and wanted to try to prove you're a man and get back at me. Surprised you didn't need someone to hold your hand, being out here in the dark all by yourself. Do you need someone to help you get it up, too, you pussy?"

She heard movement and jumped to the side of the door just as it was flung open. Red Shirt had Eve by the throat and was using her as a shield. Elle barely registered that Eve's shirt had been torn open to expose her breasts, or that she was crying. Eve stumbled forward from the force of his dramatic display. The motion put a small amount of separation between her and Red Shirt. Red Shirt had been expecting Elle to be in front of the door, and he burst out like an idiot. Rookie move. Elle darted in low, just out of Red Shirt's eyeline, and drove the blade of her knife into the exposed portion of his thigh. He screamed and lost his grip on Eve. Elle pulled her out of Red Shirt's reach.

Elle's vision was starting to narrow on Red Shirt. She hated this man. Calling over her shoulder to Eve, she said, "Run, get out of here."

"What about you?"

"Go, Eve. Now!"

She didn't turn to make sure that Eve had listened, but she thought she heard the sound of gravel crunching underfoot as she ran. This was going to end here. Red Shirt had crossed the line, and he was going to pay for it, consequences be damned. He pulled the blade from his leg and was grinning at her as though the wound was nothing to him, but it was bravado. It would slow him down, but he had her knife, and she was unarmed.

"Just you and me now, bitch. You're going to learn your place."

Elle didn't respond; she wasn't going to play his game. He was going to play hers. They began to circle each other, each watching the other's movements to gauge an attack strategy. Twice he feinted, and twice she didn't flinch. His cocky smirk faded and was replaced by a snarl. He moved in with the knife going for her torso. She twisted her body so it narrowly missed her stomach and stepped into the attack. Her left forearm slammed into the wrist that held the knife while she pivoted, swinging her right arm around at full force, and planted her elbow into his jaw. The impact was jarring, and her aggression took Red Shirt by surprise. She didn't let up. Continuing with her momentum, she locked her hands onto the pressure point in his wrist and forced him to drop the knife. Kicking it away, she barely escaped his grasp when he recovered. She danced away from him, but he'd been drinking, and his anger was flooding him with adrenaline.

He rushed her, and she couldn't stop the takedown, so she did the next best thing and kneed him in the face as he drove his shoulder into her waist. They came down at an awkward angle with Red Shirt landing on her legs. The pain was terrible, but it had to be worse for him. Fighting through it, Elle tried pulling herself free, but he clamped down hard on her left leg. Determined to stop her from escaping, he started climbing up her leg to regain control.

Rage overwhelmed her, and she began punching him in the head. She didn't stop. Everything around her disappeared into a red haze, and she only saw his face. She wanted to smash it until he was unrecognizable. Wherever he moved, she continued the attack—temple, back of the head, didn't matter. She wanted to put her fist through it. The next thing she knew, she felt a hand on her shoulder. Shrugging it off, she continued the assault. Then, arms wrapped around her and lifted her up. *No!*

Elle fought to get back to the ground for a moment before the sound of Number 7's voice finally registered. Looking around, she felt like she just woke from a dream. Sean was holding her, and 7 was standing off to the side, watching. Pain registered, and she looked at her hands. They were covered in blood. The skin on her knuckles had split, and her arms felt like they weighed a ton. Her body hurt, too, particularly her leg.

Finally, she looked on the ground and saw Red Shirt trying to push himself into a sitting position. His face was swollen and bleeding from his forehead, cheek, nose, and lip. His leg was also bleeding, and he moved very slowly. From the way he was lying, she'd managed to get the dominant position during their fight. Why couldn't she remember?

Taking deep breaths in and out to calm her racing pulse and putting her hands up in a conciliatory way, she said, "Let me go. I'm all right."

7 nodded, and Sean let her go. Elle pushed her hair out of her face and tried to straighten up as much as possible.

"What are you doing here, Gerard? I can handle this on my own," Elle said.

"Thought I would come and see how things played out for myself," he said.

"Is this a problem?"

"Actually, I was going to ask you the same thing."

"I'll take care of it. As far as I'm concerned, he's lucky to be alive. If you had been just a few minutes longer, I wouldn't have to deal with him anymore."

"I can remedy that for you."

This is it. The final test. If she didn't play this right, it was game over. Elle looked over at Red Shirt. He was watching them, and she could see fear set in. His life was in her hands, and everything in her wanted him dead. "And what would that cost me?"

"You."

"Excuse me?"

"Leave your team and work for me."

"No. Wait! Don't trust this bitch!"

Sean kicked Red Shirt in the face and pulled his gun on him.

Looking over Gerard's shoulder, Elle saw Eve standing in the doorway of the hotel. Elle could see her clutching her torn shirt together, and her rage surged. "Done."

Gerard nodded at Sean and, without hesitation, the man put two bullets in Red Shirt's head.

Elle was numb. Her mind struggled to accept what had just happened. Forcing herself to stay in role, she turned back to 7. "Now what?"

"Now, you go get cleaned up and meet me back at the penthouse."

Elle looked down and saw blood splatter everywhere. The contrast of all that red against the white suit made everything even more surreal. Nodding, she said, "What about the body?"

"Don't worry about it. Within the hour, no one will know he was ever here."

Nodding, Elle started walking over to Eve. Her legs felt wobbly, but she managed to keep them moving in the right direction. Eve was frozen in place, almost like she didn't see Elle coming. Gripping Eve's arm, Elle was surprised to see a tremor in her hand. *Post-fight adrenaline dump, that's all.* "Are you okay? Do you need a doctor?"

Tears were in Eve's eyes, and she let out a short laugh that sounded close to hysterics. "I don't know. They killed him, didn't they?"

"Yes."

Eve collapsed against the door frame and slid down to the floor, her breathing ragged. "Oh, my god, it's all my fault."

Elle crouched down and grabbed Eve's shoulders. "None of this is your fault. It's all on him. But we need to go now. We can't stay here."

Eve paled even more and looked toward the pool house. 7 and Sean were still by the body, but they wouldn't be for long. Elle helped Eve get to her feet and guided her back to their suite. The second they crossed the threshold, Elle yelled for help.

Jack ran to them. "What happened?"

"Red Shirt. I need you to get Tex and Julian back here immediately," Elle ordered.

He nodded and ran to get his phone. Elle took Eve to her room and sat her on the bed.

"Talk to me, kid."

Silence.

"Eve. Please. Let me know how to help you."

Eve shifted and looked up at her. The despair in her eyes made Elle want blood all over again. "I just wanted to check on him. He'd been gone for so long, I didn't think—"

"Stop right there. This is not your fault in any way. It's all on that piece of shit. I'm just sorry I didn't get there sooner."

"If it wasn't for you.... Thank you, Elle." Tears started streaming down Eve's face again. This time she lost the battle with her emotions and began to cry openly.

Elle threw her arms around Eve and held on, trying to provide whatever comfort she could. Eve was shaking violently with each sob. Everything protective in her welled up, and she wanted to do something to take away the pain, but this was all she could do. A soft knock on the door startled them both.

"They'll be back in ten minutes," Jack said. He walked over and handed Elle a first aid kit. "Here. Looks like you might need this." He sat down next to Eve and put an arm around her. She tensed but didn't pull away.

Elle pulled off her jacket and went to Eve's bathroom to wash her hands. The image in the mirror was shocking. It looked like she had just walked off the set of a horror movie. Washing off as much of the blood as she could, Elle wet a washcloth, grabbed a clean towel, and returned to Eve. "What hurts?"

Regaining some composure, Eve responded, "The back of my head and my neck, and I'm pretty sure I have cuts and bruises on my back and legs."

Elle moved to check the back of her head, but Eve stopped her. "Could you have stopped them?"

Unable to meet her eyes, Elle kept fussing with the first aid supplies. "I don't know. I can't change what happened. All I can do is use it."

"You can't be serious? They killed Robert in cold blood. You can't go back there," Eve said.

Shock made Jack stammer, "W-wait, what? Robert's dead?

Elle ignored him and focused on Eve. "It's my way into 7's operation. It's why we came here. I'm not stopping now."

"But he was one of us," Jack said.

"He was never one of us! And after tonight, I'm glad he's dead."

"Elle, please don't say things like that," Eve said.

Her anger boiled over. "You've got to be kidding me? He attacked you, Eve, and you guys are acting like I'm the bad guy. You know what, never mind. I don't have time for this shit right now." Throwing the first aid kit at Jack, she stood and said, "When Tex and Julian get back, start making plans to leave. You're all going home. I'll go it on my own from here on out."

Eve called after her, "Elle, wait!"

But she was gone.

Going to her room, she slammed the door. After pacing the floor for a few moments, her anger ebbed, and she regained her composure. Elle ripped off the rest of the bloody clothes and tossed them in a trash bag. Jumping in the shower, she watched as the water took on a pink tint as it cascaded from her body. Sharp stinging sensations called her attention to her knuckles. *Damnit.* She hated fight bite. She spent a few minutes really cleaning out those wounds since bacteria from the human mouth could cause a severe infection.

Not certain what else this night would throw at her, Elle chose a more practical outfit. She dressed in dark slacks and a blouse then accessorized with a knife inside her sleeve, and a second blade on her calve. She remembered the key that 7 had given her earlier and put it in her pants pocket. Feeling as ready as she was going to be, she set off to link up with 7. Walking through the suite, she could hear her team, but no one was waiting to question her further. They were likely preoccupied with the fallout of what Red Shirt had done and the orders to leave. Elle felt a huge weight lift as she slipped into the hallway. *It's better this way.*

. . .

A new Range Rover was waiting for them at the entrance of the hotel. The valet opened the passenger door for her as 7 walked around to the driver's side. Nighttime masked some of the squalor that's so prevalent in Djibouti City, hiding much of the dirt that covered everything. And the water looked cool and

147

clear. They drove in comfortable silence, just listening to the music coming through the speakers. It took her a while to place it, but she couldn't help but see the irony once she realized it was the soundtrack from the TV series *Game of Thrones*.

She had no idea where they were going until 7 turned into the main entrance of the Port of Djibouti. There was a little shack with a Djiboutian security guard standing next to two Chinese sailors. The contrast between them was absolute. The Djiboutian was very dark-skinned, frail thin, and wearing a light-blue shirt and dark pants. While being an official uniform, it looked a little threadbare and in need of washing. On the other hand, the Chinese men were pristine in white uniforms, slender but healthy, and held themselves with a rigid formality.

7 barely slowed down. As soon as the guard, who looked bored more than anything, recognized the vehicle, he raised the metal bar that served as a security blockade across the narrow entrance. The Chinese sentries glanced their way but didn't appear to pay them more than a passing interest. The tinted windows of the Range Rover prevented them from seeing inside the vehicle regardless.

Given the amount of money pouring through this port, it should have been a top-of-the-line facility, but it was the opposite. Everything inside the port was rusted, broken, and in complete disrepair. The buildings looked

T H E   D E E P E R   S H A D O W

like they could topple from strong wind, and the trucks and cargo beds looked ready to crumble into dust. Despite the appearance, port workers were all around them. They parted slowly for the Rover, the headlights revealing them to be a ragged crew that seemed to be wandering aimlessly more than anything. Even the road they were driving on seemed to be coated in a thick layer of grime.

Driving to the far end of the port, they parked in front of a seemingly abandoned building. When Elle got out of the vehicle, she was assaulted by a horrendous stench. Covering her nose, she looked around for the source.

"That ship pulling up to the pier is transporting livestock. The ships pack them in as tight as they can get them, and usually lose a few because of it. You never get used to the smell, though, no matter how many times you're around it. It's strong enough that the sharks will follow the boat into the port. They know the carcasses will be pushed overboard, and sometimes they lose a live one as they offload. One way or the other, it's a free meal."

Two men rushed over to 7. He pulled a bag of green leaves out of the back seat and tossed it at them before they got too close. "Keep everyone away," he ordered. They both nodded and gave 7 a brown-stained grin.

"How can you trust a couple of addicts?" Elle asked.

149

"It's not about trust. Their addiction will win out over anything else. The only thing I want from them is to disappear somewhere far from here. They'll run off with the khat and be high in no time. Word will spread that they have a bag of leaves, and all attention will go to them and away from us."

Turning toward the building, he gestured for her to follow. Elle grimaced. She didn't even want to think about what she was walking on. She could feel the grime under her shoes. As they rounded the corner of the building, she saw it was the last in a line of several identical structures.

"After the conflict in Yemen started, this became a refugee camp of sorts. These buildings were used as barracks to house them until they were sent elsewhere." He unlocked the door and went inside.

There were rows of empty bunk beds on either side of a narrow isle running down the room's center. It felt as though no one had been there in some time. There was a layer of dust on everything, and several of the bunks were toppled over. As her eyes adjusted, she saw a clear path on the floor running to the far side of the room where there was a metal cabinet. As they got closer to it, she realized it was a façade. It looked like every other cheap metal cabinet favored by government agencies, but the lock was hefty and new. Touching the door, she could feel that it was made from a thick steel plate instead of a cheap composite.

"I'm assuming there is something of value in here."

"Probably. You wanted to know what your key was for." He looked at the lock.

Taking the key out of her pocket, Elle opened the lock and marveled at the door's thickness and the ease with which it opened. Looking inside, she was surprised to see a staircase heading underground. 7 stepped through the cabinet doors onto the stairs and looked at her expectantly. She followed without question. As soon as she was beside him, he closed the doors, and there was an audible click of the lock re-engaging. There was a moment of pitch-black before red lights came on to assist with their decent.

Elle followed 7 down at least fifteen feet to a short hallway with another door. This one had a hand scanner on the wall. He placed his hand on the screen, which turned green after a few seconds, unlocking the door. As soon as he pushed it open, lights turned on, revealing an armory. There were several black, leather chairs in what appeared to be a viewing area that looked out over the deadliest "show floor" she had ever seen. Weapons of all kinds were showcased in lighted, stainless-steel display cases, with large, black drawers under them that, no doubt, held more weaponry. She never imagined something like this would exist outside Hollywood.

Walking through the room, she was amazed by the number of weapons this man had accumulated. He had every type she could think of. No wonder he hadn't been concerned with losing merchandise. His business was massive and obviously extremely successful. There was no need to fake the awe she felt, and she knew it showed on her face. "This is incredible."

"I've been working toward this for the last ten years. Cultivating all the right connections, building leverage, and a client base, removing the competition. But I'm always looking for a new edge."

"Like what?"

"Like you."

"What are you talking about?"

He squared off in front of her.

Elle could feel the heat coming off his body.

"I looked into you before you arrived, and you've exceeded my expectations since we met. You are a stunningly beautiful woman, ruthless, and more than capable of handling yourself. I want to bring you on to be the face of my business, to meet the clients, and make the sales. I can think of nothing sexier than you with a weapon in your hands, and, since clients tend to be men, I can see my sales increasing just because they want to deal with you."

"You want me to be your sex symbol?"

He laughed. "There's no denying that sex sells, but it's much more than that, and I think you know it. This business is volatile and extremely dangerous. Only the smart and lethal succeed. Every meeting could go bad, and every client could be trying to kill or double-cross you. It happens more often than not."

"So, you're offering me a chance to become a target?"

"I'm offering you a never-ending adventure. Constant challenges with deadly consequences and living life to its fullest." With a low voice, he added, "Complete freedom. And all the excitement and pleasure that goes with it." His hand found the button of her blouse and opened it slowly, giving her the chance to say no.

She didn't.

"You make an intriguing proposal. Being on your team is one thing, but I'm not sure I want that kind of attention. I'll consider it." Elle stepped away and removed her blouse casually, exposing the sheathed knife on her forearm. As she laid the blouse on one of the chairs, she watched as 7 eyed her hungrily. Her being armed seemed to excite him more. She could feel the weight of his gaze and became hyperaware of the fact that they were very much alone. Looking around the viewing area, she found a small Bose stereo system and turned it on. Marilyn Manson started to play. She assumed they regularly invited women here to entertain their clientele, because this song's rhythm was straight seduction. Elle embraced it.

She walked back to 7, placed her hands on his shoulders, and swayed her hips to the music, coaxing him into a dance. He didn't hesitate. His hands found her waist and pulled her body against his. The dance fanned the flames between them, building to impossible levels. Elle was lost in the moment, and she loved it. 7 pulled his shirt off before his hands found her pants' button and pushed them down off her hips. He groaned in pleasure when he saw the second blade on her leg. This increased her excitement even further and earned him a passionate kiss. Removing the last of their clothing, Elle backed him into a nearby chair and straddled him. She lost herself in the heat of the moment, taking her pleasure. He was more than ready to oblige her.

Elle lost track of time, but eventually, her mind returned her to the present. Somehow, they ended up on the floor. The sweat on her body had cooled enough that she was starting to shiver, despite the body heat still radiating from Gerard, who was lying next to her. Getting to her feet, she stretched languidly and started gathering her clothes.

He watched her with an amused look before he joined her in dressing, chuckling to himself.

"What?" she asked.

"I'm no stranger to casual sex, belle. But this is different. We have such chemistry, but you seem as though you could walk away from me at any time. It's a bit of a strange experience for me."

Elle shrugged. "Emotions are a liability. We have fun. Why not just enjoy the rush and leave it at that?"

He laughed. "A woman after my own heart."

As she adjusted her hair, Elle walked around the room, studying every detail of the layout and the displays. Coming to a section that looked different from the others, she studied the hardware for a moment before reaching out and running her hands along the edges of a shelf. She could see Gerard watching her with a silent look of approval.

Elle found what she was looking for and pressed a button. With a snap, a latch released, and she pulled outward on the shelf. The wall moved to reveal a storage area that was almost as big as the room they were in. It was stacked with weapons and ammunition crates. There had to be millions of dollars of merchandise in there. Elle whistled at the sight.

She felt his arms circle around her waist and pull her back against him. "I knew I was right about you. Have you finished considering my proposal?"

"I have, but I need some time." Turning in his arms, she said, "I can't just walk away without finishing the jobs I've already taken. Or making arrangements for them to go on without me."

"That's acceptable. It will give me some time to inform the others that you're coming on board. You showed your worth on the *Black Eagle,* and again tonight with your hand-to-hand skills, but there are always issues with new faces."

"Understandable. So, what do we do now?"

His smile was pure sin. "I have you all to myself right now. So, I'm going to take advantage of the time while I have it."

CHAPTER 13

Sunlight woke Elle. It took her a minute to remember that she was back in Gerard's suite. Looking over, she saw that he was still asleep next to her. Moving carefully to avoid waking him, she located her clothes and began to dress so she could make her escape.

Soft laughter alerted her that he was awake. "You really know how to shake a man's confidence."

"I doubt anything could scratch yours."

"True. Until I met you." He got out of bed and walked over to her, completely comfortable with his nudity. Wrapping his arms around her, he said, "I think we'll be an amazing team."

Elle's stomach flipped, and there was a rush of excitement. When she was with Gerard, she felt free. No pain, no memories, no emotions tearing her apart. It was all sensation and action—what she needed and craved more than anything. Maybe she could draw this out a little longer. She didn't need to rush.

"It'll take some time to figure out what my next move is."

"Come back tonight. The team will be here, and we can get started."

"I still have work to do, and technically I haven't accepted your offer yet."

"Perhaps my confidence is still intact after all. If the proposal alone isn't enticing enough, I'm counting on my charm to win you over."

"You have charm? I hadn't noticed." Elle kissed him deeply. When she pulled away, she finished dressing and said, "I suppose you have some appeal." With that, she left him standing there and returned to her suite.

It was very early in the morning, and the hotel was silent. Walking into the kitchen, she grabbed water and stood by the sink drinking. Elle was so wrapped up in her thoughts, measuring out the possibilities of just saying to hell with everything and taking the offer, she didn't notice she wasn't alone. Looking by the windows in the living room, her heart stopped beating when she saw Julian sitting in one of the chairs, a coffee, and newspaper on the table beside him. He was just watching her. Guilt hit her like a sledgehammer.

Forcing herself to smile, she said, "I figured everyone would still be asleep."

"I couldn't really sleep. So, I thought I would relax here, waiting for you."

Knots almost made her stomach cramp. What the hell was wrong with her? Elle had no doubt he wanted to talk about more than the mission. He looked relaxed, but she could feel the tension behind his calm demeanor. She stalled, trying to get herself together. "How's Eve?"

"Tex was able to get the Embassy doctor to see her first thing. Jack went with them."

Anger helped settle the churning in her stomach enough to feel a little more in control. "I never should have let him anywhere near Eve."

"It was a hard choice in a tough situation."

"It should have never happened!" Elle snapped.

Julian's brow creased, and he studied her face. "You can't control everything, Elle. No matter how much you want to."

"I don't need a sermon."

"Not giving you one."

For a long time, Elle stood there, feeling the weight of his gaze. She knew what he saw. Hair and clothes slightly rumpled, coming in so early in the morning after being out all night. She couldn't shake the feeling of guilt. *I don't owe him any explanations.*

Finally, he asked, "How's the mission going?"

"Not quite as planned, but what happened last night sealed the deal. I'm on the inside and being shown everything. It's awe-inspiring. This is a massive operation, and it's been very carefully built."

"It must be. You sound like a fan."

"It's just business. Gerard is brilliant and runs a very tight operation."

"Gerard?"

It took a few seconds for the implications of what she had just said to hit. She was speechless. The blood rushing through her ears, overwhelmed her other senses. Gerard, not Number 7. When had he stopped being a target? Minutes earlier, she had been considering her target's offer. She was so shaken that she didn't realize Julian had moved until he was right next to her. She wanted to argue, deny everything that single slip of the tongue alleged, but she couldn't find the words. Julian's gaze held her captive. She felt like she was falling. Reaching out, he brushed a stray hair from her face.

"This can't be what you want. You need to bow out before there's no turning back."

She felt sick. She didn't want to deal with this. "I don't need you to tell me what to do, and it's none of your business. My decisions are mine, and I don't need your approval or permission."

"So, you're going to support Daesh now?" His words rocked her harder than any punch could have. As a wave of nausea hit, she swore that the floor moved under her feet.

He didn't ease up, "Deny it all you want, you can't hide from the truth. You're compromised. If you choose to run with Gerard, your mission fails. You would be helping supply Daesh and every other psychopath out there with money and the weapons they use to commit murder. Innocent people will die."

Desperate denials roared through her head. Her stomach cramped so hard she had to grip the sink to keep her knees from buckling, choking back the water that was trying to come up her throat. Impossible, this could not be happening. *Never.*

"You need to be clear on this: Tex, Eve, Jack…me, we would be on the opposite side. We know who and what you are. So, are you going to take us all out to keep your new position? Or are you going to have Gerard do it, so you have deniability?"

Elle couldn't think, could barely breathe. It had felt so amazing, the absolute freedom. She could feel the pull even now, but it wasn't real. It was like a drug, just another painkiller that destroyed more than helped. *How did I let this happen?* Despair crept in for the first time since she left the hospital, and tears burned in her eyes. Refusing to let Julian see them, she pushed away from the sink and moved to her room on shaky legs.

He didn't try to stop her.

Closing the door, Elle suddenly couldn't stand the feel of her clothes and pulled them off, nearly ripping the seams in her haste. Moving to the bathroom, she turned on the shower and climbed under the hot water. Tears started streaming down her face, and sobs racked her body. She dropped to the floor and cried openly as the hot water beat down on her. She was an emotional wreck again. Despair, anger, fear, anxiety, and frustration all vied for dominance. She was trapped in her own mind, intermittently blaming herself and others for her failure.

Elle had no idea how long she sat on the shower floor, but her muscles started to ache from the trembling. Whether it was from the force of crying or because she'd been sitting there for so long, she couldn't tell. Slowly getting to her feet to avoid becoming lightheaded or slipping, she turned off the faucet and got out. Looking at herself in the mirror was disturbing. Her skin was red from the hot water beating down on it for so long, her face was blotchy, and her eyes were swollen. Completely drained, Elle left the bathroom and sat on the bed. There was no longer any question in her mind that she had changed, and there was no going back.

She felt adrift.

Grabbing her phone, she typed an encrypted message to Dr. Wise: *I failed.*

A few minutes later, the phone rang. She hesitated before answering but knew this conversation was inevitable.

"Are you able to talk freely, Elle?" Wise asked.

"I don't want to talk at all, but yeah, I'm alone."

"How much time do you have?"

"Just get on with it, Doc. This line may be encrypted, but I don't want to keep it open."

"Okay. Well, at least this isn't going to be as bad as I thought," Wise said.

Confused, Elle asked, "Why would you say that?"

"You're still thinking about the security of your operation, that shows you're still in the game."

Elle was stunned and couldn't think of how to respond for a moment. "Habit, I guess."

"No. Instinct. So, unless you're telling me that your cover has been blown, you're still in this."

"I've lost control of the situation, Doc, and a man died."

"I read about the KIA. The report said he was killed by one of your target's men. Is that true?"

"Yes, but—"

"Could you have stopped it without being exposed?"

"What?"

"You heard me. I have no doubt that you could have saved that man, so the real question is, could you have done it without exposing yourself and your team?"

Elle felt off balance. *That's not the question you should be asking, Doc.* "I don't know."

"If you can't say yes without hesitation, then it wasn't within your ability to control. Regardless of the circumstances."

Elle thought about what he said. She'd wanted Red Shirt dead, but, if she hadn't, could she have saved him without compromising the mission? Scenario after scenario ran through her head, none of them good. *Is Wise right, or is he just handling me?* "I know you're going to say whatever's necessary to keep me in the game. I get it. You chose me, and no one wants to prove that I was worth the risk more than me. But things have gone so far off track, I don't know what I'm supposed to do."

"That's entirely up to you. If you truly feel like you can't continue, then stop. Your options are: let someone else take the lead on your mission, kill the target, or finish what you started. The choice is yours to make. But, before you decide, there's something you need to know: you're the third agent to try and take down this target."

"We didn't see any reports on other ops," Elle said.

"Because they weren't ours. They were MI6. The first one never made it past the entourage. The second agent had been in deep cover for years, but Gerard Fior made him before he could make any headway identifying the suppliers. They never found the body."

"How did we find out about this?" Elle asked.

"Pure chance. The Station Chief just sat in on an update from an interagency task force on weapons trafficking through the Horn of Africa. The British liaison commented about the level of the threat in DJ that made it seem as though they were speaking from experience. They called in a few favors and got the details. You've made it further than anyone ever has, or likely will again."

"So, your experiment worked. The PTSD made my cover real. But here's the problem, being broken may have gotten me further than anyone else, but what good is that when I can't trust myself?"

Wise sighed. "You sound exhausted, Elle. I have an idea on how to help you. But, first, you need to rest. Get as much sleep as you can right now. When you wake up, the only thing I want you to think about is what you want to do. Not what you think you should do, or what's expected of you, what you actually want. You need to be all in with whatever your decision is."

"Sure, Doc. Whatever you say." Elle hung up, feeling conflicted and more drained than before. Crawling into the bed, she worked to clear her mind. *What do I want?*

Hunger woke her. She was startled to see that, not only had she fallen asleep, she had been out for hours. It was mid-afternoon, and no one had disturbed her. Getting up, she felt like she was on autopilot. She returned to the shower to wash and then got dressed. The entire time her head revolved around a single train of thought. *What do I want?* Every choice felt uncomfortable in some way. She was struggling. Wise was right, though. One way or the other, the choice was hers to make.

A knock on the door broke her train of thought.

Clearing her throat, she called out permission to enter.

Tex walked in, looking uncertain. "You doing okay, Mama?"

"Truth? I don't know."

He closed the door and sat in the chair by the window. "Talk to me."

"Wise called you, didn't he?"

"Yeah. He said you needed me, but you were passed out hard when I got back. So, I've just been keeping an eye on you, waiting for you to wake up."

Shit. Elle hung her head in her hands. Her mind reeled, and she blurted out, "What the hell is wrong with me? The devil made me an offer. I was going to take it, and a man died because of that. What kind of person does that? Turns against everything that truly matters?"

"Bullshit. You haven't turned against anything. You're human, Elle. No matter how hard you try to convince everyone you're not. You've been through hell, and no one gets out of that unscathed. So, you got tempted by the dark side, who hasn't? I've heard they have cookies."

Elle rolled her eyes, but his attempt to lighten the mood did ease some of her tension. "I'm being serious, Mike."

"So am I, Elle. You wouldn't be raking yourself over the coals right now if you were already a lost cause. I know you hated the guy, and after what he did to Eve,

I'm not sorry that he's dead. But, you didn't pull the trigger, and you're not God."

"How is she?" Elle asked.

"Physically? Just some cuts and bruises. Last night scared the hell out of her. She's shaken up but pushing through. We all are. I've talked to the team, and we're all in agreement; we're still with you. But the next move is yours. Are you sending us away? Are we getting back to work?"

It's all on me. The pressure to choose felt like it was crushing her. "I'm going to finish the mission. I have to. Any move I make outside of that will leave me questioning myself."

Nodding, Tex stood and pulled her to her feet. "Then let's get back to it."

"That easy?" Elle asked.

"None of this has been easy, Elle. If it was, anyone could do it. But we have a chance to make a real impact. That's worth fighting for. And so are you. The stuff that matters always is."

Elle's throat constricted, and her eyes burned. Turning away, she said, "Okay. Let's do this. Give me some time to collect my thoughts. I'll meet you out there."

He hesitated.

"I promise. I'm coming."

"You better be. We need you." Tex shut the door behind him as he left the room.

Standing by the window, Elle forced her thoughts to the task at hand. It wasn't easy, but eventually, her focus returned. She ran over every detail of the last couple of days, and, before she knew it, she was ready. She took a few more breaths, inhaling and exhaling, to steady herself before facing her team, and left the room.

They were sitting around the dining table, viewing something on Jack's laptop.

"Bring me up to speed."

There was an almost audible sigh of relief from Eve before she began. "There's been a lot of interest in the file we created referencing the Fior Network. Jack has been monitoring when it's accessed: four times since last night."

"I also gave myself a backdoor into the hotel's camera system."

Elle raised an eyebrow at Jack's disclosure.

He shrugged. "I was bored, and their IT guy sucks. Anyway, there's a camera outside the penthouse. I've watched a few guys go in there over the last hour. I think we got their attention."

Elle felt her raw emotions abate. The plan was working to perfection, despite her lack of focus. It was now or never. "There's going to be a meeting tonight with all of 7's crew." She put emphasis on the number and met Julian's eyes when she did. It was essential for them all to know she was going to see this thing through. "Things are going to get heated fast. I'll get blamed for the leak initially, but it won't hold. Eventually, we're going to move to the weapons cache at the port. Jack, how are you with biometric locks?"

"Hand or eye?"

"Hand."

"That's doable as long as he didn't clean the scanner the last time he touched it."

"Is there any way to guard against him being notified that the location has been entered? I didn't see anything, but my gut tells me he has it monitored somehow."

Jack thought for a moment, "If you didn't see anything, that probably rules out video surveillance. Which just leaves electronic alerts, probably cellular. Since there's only the one cell network here, I think I can disrupt it long enough to get us in and out, but the alert will eventually go through. He'll know someone was there."

"I'll take it. Be ready to move as soon as possible. You, Tex, and Julian will be going in as soon as it's dark enough to provide screening. Tex, give yourself plenty of time to lose any surveillance and locate a way to break into the port undetected. I'll walk you through the layout, the security situation, and where the weapons are located. I would avoid anything that has to do with swimming. You don't want to be in that water."

"Got it. What are we doing once we're in there?"

"Plant the GPS trackers. I need you to tag the most lucrative cargo. Treat it like you would if it were the intended mission. We need to make sure that it feels real. Take a few pictures of the tagged cargo. Jack, once we have those pictures, break back into the jihadist forums and any black sites you can slip into without leaving a trail. I want you to post them as though they were leaked intelligence showing this network has been compromised and that the weapons are being tracked. Get the word out that receiving them is a trap. Eve will be here ready to assist with the posts when you get back, and Julian will be your eyes and ears while you're inside." Turning to Julian, she asked, "How's your aim these days?"

He gave her a crooked smile. "I can hit the broad side of a barn two out of three times, easy. What do you need me to do?"

"I need you to set up a sniper position at the port and dig in. You'll be overwatch for the boys as they do their thing, but then I need you to stay in place to engage a target later. The shot will need to be perfectly placed to create a wound but give the appearance that it was intended to kill. And then you'll need to exfil ASAP. These guys will come after you if they can ID point of origin. You and Tex work out a rally location."

Julian looked confused. "You want me to just wound the guy?"

"I'm the target."

Julian looked stunned as Eve gasped, "Elle, you can't be serious?"

"I may be getting pretty good at it, but I'm not a fan of being shot. So, yes, I'm serious."

"What's the play?" Tex asked.

"Pull up current imagery of the port, Jack. Tonight we finish this."

CHAPTER 14

Back in her red suit, Elle walked through the halls of the hotel toward the penthouse ready for battle. Her emotions were at war with each other, but her resolve held. This was her choice. Reaching the door, she braced to see 7 again. Time to put all her skills to the test. She rang the bell and feigned surprise when Max answered. He didn't smile but inclined his head before stepping back to let her in. The whole team was seated around the living room, all with somber expressions. Number 7 sat in a chair at the head of it all. He looked angry.

Elle glanced at each man in turn, and then at 7. "I take it something is amiss?"

"I bet it's her," Drake snarled.

That didn't take long. "What's me?"

7 cleared his throat. "It would seem that someone has been unhappy with the way things are and has started planning to take me down."

"Did you know about this before you asked me to join your team, Gerard?"

The room erupted with variations of "what the fuck?" though Drake seemed the most outraged.

"Enough!" 7's sharp command sliced through the uproar. He got to his feet, looking every inch a man capable of breaking skulls, if pressed. "This is my business, and I will run it how I see fit. Is that clear?" There was no doubt from his tone that the question was rhetorical. Pacing past each of them, he said, "Someone in this room is a traitor. Our last venture displeased them enough to finally take action. Now, the CIA is building a case to take me down."

"It's your little whore, Gerard. Or is it just a coincidence that this happened after she showed up..." Drake said.

Elle eyed him coolly. "I can't think of anyone in this group less displeased than you were on that ship, Drake. Seems like you're pushing this a little too hard. You chose wrong if you were looking for an easy scapegoat."

"Fuck you, bitch."

Elle met Rhen's gaze levelly. "You might want to wrangle your boy before he hurts himself."

Rhen's eyes darkened with anger, but Elle's attention pulled back to Drake when he sprang to his feet and moved toward her. Elle squared off ready to fight, but Sean and Max were between them in an instant. They pushed Drake away, telling him to back off as Rhen pulled him back to his seat, whispering something. He was furious, but whatever Rhen said had influenced him to stay put.

Number 7 had watched the interaction speculatively. He was more than willing to let them all kill each other if that meant outing the traitor and salvaging his business. She almost wanted to thank him. All the emotions that had been tearing her up inside settled. This man had no loyalty other than to himself. She'd made the right choice. Smiling, she moved to his side. "Well, this isn't quite the reception I had anticipated tonight, but things are definitely never boring with you."

He returned her smile, but it didn't reach his eyes. "This isn't what I had intended either, belle. But we can still make the best of it."

Chase leaned forward then. "We? Gerard, you can't be serious about bringing this woman in. We barely know her. Drake has a point. We didn't have problems until she arrived. We can't trust her."

"Actually, Chase, she's one of only two people in this room who I think I can trust isn't the traitor."

"Then, please, listen to me when I say you need to be cautious," Chase said.

"And why should I do that? You aren't the other person I'm talking about."

Chase looked shocked. "You can't possibly think that I would ever betray you?"

"I think everyone has their price. You know that I have eyes and ears well placed to warn me when something is threatening my business. I may have gotten notified later than I would have preferred, but it's better late than never. For the last six months, someone in this group has been meeting with an agent from the CIA. Given that piece of information alone, it means that Elle and Max are the only two people who do not fit the profile."

Heads turned to look at Max, who went from looking relieved to very uncomfortable once the attention was on him. Trying to be nonchalant, he said, "So, what do we do now, Gerard?"

"Find out who's betraying me and deal with them, of course. I've been narrowing it down ever since I received my first report."

"To who?" Luke asked.

"To those who I can't account for when this last meeting with the CIA took place. Which only leaves Chase, Rhen, Drake, and Sean. So, gentlemen, where were you the afternoon after we visited to the *Black Eagle*?" He looked at them each, in turn, waiting for answers.

"I went home, Gerard. And I didn't go anywhere until you called me," Chase replied.

"Drake and I went out to Menelik Square to blow off some steam," Rhen said.

Drake gave a curt nod in agreement.

Sean leaned forward and said, "I was here in the hotel. I had those two ladies waiting for me when we got back. Didn't get out of bed to do more than piss until late in the afternoon. You have to be able to verify that. I was still here when you called last night."

"Verifying that will be easy. The question then becomes, what were you talking about with those ladies?"

Sean paled.

7 continued, "Unfortunately, that wasn't as helpful as I had hoped. Any of you could be lying. So, we're back to square one."

"How confident are you in your information?" Elle asked.

"Very. The information is too accurate to be fabricated or coincidence."

"Care to share with the group?" Rhen asked.

7 gave him a hard stare for a moment before shrugging. "After I made the decision to liquidate most of the cargo the pirates had taken, our traitor decided that was the final blow. He just couldn't take losing out on a payday and thinks himself smarter than me. So, he decided to double-dip. I pay him for his services, while the CIA also pays him to place trackers on my shipments, so they can intercept them and build a case against me."

"Sounds like a bunch of bullshit to me," Drake muttered.

"For once, dipshit over there may be onto something," Elle said.

All eyes turned toward her, and Drake gave her the finger.

"It sounds too neat," Elle continued. "And shortsighted. Like something you would say to a mark to get paid. Wouldn't be the first time someone sold a line to the CIA to get them to reach into their pocketbook and shell out some money for information. Have you checked to see if there's any proof? Otherwise, you just have suspicion and conjecture."

They all turned to 7. He was still eyeing Drake and Rhen. There was no indication he even heard her until he said, "Let's find out. Shall we? A little field trip to the showroom. Anyone interested in seeing this for themselves should come." The implication in his cavalier statement was plain—he expected the guilty party to run. He turned to Chase and whispered something. Chase's face was unreadable, but he gave a slight nod.

With a smile, 7 turned around and offered his arm.

Elle took it and walked with him to the door without another word.

The others followed.

As they rode alone in the elevator, Elle leaned into 7 and said, "You certainly know how to keep a girl on her toes."

His arms went around her. Pulling her tightly in, he looked into her eyes.

What she saw was a barely contained rage.

"There will be blood tonight. No one betrays me."

"You have more problems than that, and I think you know it."

He scowled. "What do you mean?"

"Rhen and Drake are only half your problem. Chase's the other."

There was a long silence before he said, "I'm not surprised that you picked up on my main concern. But what the hell are you talking about with Chase?"

"He's obsessed with you. His whole world revolves around being your 'go-to' guy, and he's a little territorial of that relationship. It's not going to be too much longer before he starts making decisions for your own good or weeding out what he sees as competition." She paused before she asked, "Is he gay?"

7's face twisted in distaste. "No. That's ridiculous."

Elle shrugged. "If you say so, but something is off there. I would be careful. Perhaps you should consider a clean break too."

When they reached the ground floor, Elle saw the valet had already brought 7's vehicle. Looking around, she didn't see the other men, but several other vehicles were waiting behind the Range Rover. Number 7 didn't wait to see who would follow him. He moved to the driver's side as Elle climbed into the passenger seat. Once again, there was instrumental music playing. She couldn't place where it came from, but it was dark, which suited the mood.

They rode to the port in silence. Elle lounged in her seat, appearing at ease as she scanned the terrain, periodically checking the side mirror for any sign of trouble. Arriving first, they sat in the vehicle waiting for the others. Three other vehicles pulled in next to them. Rhen and Drake rode together. Sean, Max, and Luke shared a ride also. The last car to pull up held Chase. 7 seemed disappointed that everyone had shown, but he led them into the building with another nod to Chase. Everyone but Chase followed.

Elle wasn't the only one who'd noticed.

"Why isn't Chase coming in?" Rhen asked.

"I've asked him to make sure no one unexpected joins us."

"How do you know he's not your fucking narc?" Drake accused.

"Call it a calculated risk. If I'm wrong, we'll know soon enough," 7 replied coldly.

Entering the building, Elle watched for any hints that her team had run into issues. She had been out of communications with them since they left the hotel suite, so she had no choice but to trust that everything was ready. Nothing appeared any different from the last time she had been here.

She walked confidently beside 7 to the hidden entrance. Before he opened the lock, 7 glanced at his cell phone and scowled.

"What's wrong?" she asked.

"My security system logs and notifies me every time someone accesses my showroom. The cell network was down earlier, so I didn't get any notices, but it appears to be functioning again."

"Did someone get in?"

"It shows the last person to enter was me, but the time is wrong. It says it was only an hour ago."

"I guess we'll see soon enough if you have a system error or if your security has been compromised."

The look on 7's face promised death, but he didn't respond to her. He opened the first lock, and they all moved into the stairwell. The main door was locked, and it opened as expected when 7 placed his hand on the scanner. Inside the showroom, everything was exactly as it had been yesterday. Guilt flared for a moment when she thought about that visit, but she forced it away. It was game time.

7 didn't slow once he entered the showroom and walked directly to the hidden room. Opening the door, he stood back to watch them as he said, "Break into teams and search every crate. Luke and Sean start in the back. Drake, you're with me, starting here. Elle, you're with Rhen and Max. Start going through all the merchandise on the floor. Search every inch of this place."

Elle saw Rhen's jaw clench, but he didn't openly protest. Drake was the weak link in their team, and both Rhen and 7 knew it.

With a little reluctance, Rhen turned to them. "Let's get this charade over with. I say we start with the pieces that are hardest to obtain."

"The .50 cals?" Max asked.

"It's as good a place to start as any," Rhen replied.

Moving to the main wall, they all started to search the drawers and the showpieces on display. They were halfway around the room before they heard a loud crash and a barrage of curses in French. Elle could see where Number 7 had flipped over a crate of rifles through the open storeroom door. There was a GPS tracker in his hand. The crate had a false bottom that opened when it was overturned. It was filled with cash.

"Search every fucking crate! I want every tracker found and destroyed now!" Before anyone could blink, 7 was in Drake's face. "Did you do this? Don't fucking lie to me, you arrogant piece of shit! You've been running your mouth for months, and you're stupid enough to think you could pull off something like this."

Elle felt the tension ratchet up around her.

Drake didn't have the sense to know when to be conciliatory. Instead, he responded to 7's aggression in kind. "Get the fuck out of my face before I break you like the little bitch you are."

It happened so fast that Elle barely registered that 7 had moved. The metal glint of the brass knuckles could have been a trick of the light. The strike was quick and brutal.

Drake went down hard. The punch likely broke bones on impact and knocked the man unconscious. 7 was seething and looked at Rhen with a challenge.

Rhen didn't bite. He met 7's glare with one of his own but held his ground.

"There are a few items in the back of my Rover that I think we'll need for when Drake wakes up. It'll help make sure he answers my questions. Go get them, Rhen," 7 ordered.

Elle had no doubt that those items were restraints and probably drugs. 7 was testing Rhen. He was convinced he had his informant, and now he was fishing to see if Drake had acted alone. Inclining his head, Rhen turned and walked out.

"You sure you want him to go out alone?" Elle asked.

7 considered it for a moment, then said, "Make sure he comes back."

"No problem." She hurried to catch up to Rhen.

When Elle reached the surface, she saw Rhen as he was leaving the building. He was walking to the back of the Rover, cursing under his breath when she caught up. "You know," Elle started, "it doesn't matter what you say or do now, he's going to think you're guilty."

"So, you sleep with him, and you think you know what Gerard thinks. That's cute."

"Didn't take me sleeping with you to see that you and Drake were plotting something. If I could see it after a couple of days, there's no way Gerard missed it. The question is, what? I don't think you would do something like this. You're not an idiot. Drake would definitely do it, but I doubt he would make a move without you. So, what's your play? Or do I have it wrong, and this is all you?"

Rhen gave a short mirthless laugh. "What do you expect to have happen here? That I'll confess all my sins? Or maybe you'll offer to help me out of this mess, for a price? The question really is, what's your play?"

Elle smirked and looked at her watch. "I want the same thing I've always wanted…" She trailed off and looked around with sudden awareness. "Where's Chase?"

Rhen went still as well and began to look around. "I don't see him anywhere."

A small red light flashed across Rhen's face and settled over his heart. Elle lunged at him as she yelled, "Down!"

An all too familiar pain seared through the flesh of her left shoulder as she slammed into Rhen's chest, taking them both to the ground. When they hit, they moved behind the cover of the Rover as more bullets rained down around them. He pulled a gun from the small of his back and looked at her. "You hit?"

"It's fine. Got another gun?"

He pulled a small pistol from an ankle holster and handed it to her. "We need to find the shooter, or none of us are getting out of here."

Elle checked to make sure the gun was ready to fire. "The shot came from the south, so they'd have to be set up high to clear the buildings. If we move west, we can use the barracks as cover and work our way around. How long before the local authorities arrive?"

"This time at night, fifteen minutes. Port security can't handle anything like this, so they'll wait for police backup," Rhen answered.

"Then we need to move. I don't want to be hanging around for that." Elle didn't wait for a response; she was on her feet and running for the cover of the building. A couple of shots rang out and landed entirely too close for comfort. She felt a burn across her left thigh but didn't take another round. Adrenaline pumping hard, she paused to watch Rhen dodge several more bullets before joining her. They moved around the buildings until they had a view to the south. Cautiously, they looked at the shooter's options.

"That half-constructed building to the east has line of sight from the roof," she said.

"There's too much open ground between here and there. If we're spotted before we make it to cover, we're done."

Elle looked around and saw an old pickup truck. "How are you at hot-wiring?"

He followed her gaze and ran to the truck. Ripping open the door, he started pulling wires before she could even get around to the other side. The truck came to life with some effort, but once it got started, it stayed running. Rhen jumped behind the wheel as she got in and floored it. The force of the acceleration jarred Elle's shoulder, and she grimaced. Bracing as best as she could, she watched for any sign of movement around the buildings ahead. The windshield was filthy and restricted their field of view, but it worked for what they needed.

Rhen didn't slow as they approached the building and drove the truck right into the bottom floor, busting through the frame of what would have been the main entrance. Elle saw lights behind her eyes as her shoulder slammed into the seat, but she refused to allow the wound to distract her. Breathing through the pain, she exited the truck and backed Rhen as they found some stairs and started their climb. The structure was quiet.

They moved fast, not bothering to clear each floor. Time was crucial. If the shooter wasn't still on the roof, then only chance would allow them to catch up. Passing the fourth floor, Rhen paused at a closed door that would take them to the roof. He met her eyes, and she nodded for him to go. They cleared the door and quickly quartered the entire roof looking for the shooter. Nothing. Moving to the side the shots would have come from, they found an abandoned sniper rifle.

Grabbing the rifle, Rhen said, "We need to go. If he doubles back, he could sell any line of shit to Gerard."

Matching his stride, she said, "You think it was Chase, don't you?"

"And you don't?"

"Depends. Got anyone else that wants you dead?"

"Several of those shots were meant for you. So, can you think of anyone else who would want us both out of the way?" he asked.

They hadn't been gone for long, but it was enough that Number 7 must have gotten impatient. Max and Sean were out by the Rover on full alert after finding the bullet holes and blood from her wound. When they pulled up in the truck, both men drew their weapons. Despite coming out with their hands up, the men were worked up enough from the night's events; they held them at gunpoint until they saw she was the source of the blood. Neither man had forgotten what she had done for them on the *Black Eagle*.

Rhen brushed past them to go back into the showroom. "We need to get the hell out of here. Now."

"What happened?" Max asked.

They didn't respond.

Elle followed right behind Rhen, holding pressure on the wound to stifle the blood flow. The adrenaline rush was subsiding, and she felt a sharp twinge with each step she took. Looking down, she saw where a bullet had literally burned across her thigh. *Can't get much closer than that.*

When they reached the showroom, 7 turned around and looked stunned by what he saw. Rhen threw the rifle on the floor and spoke before anyone else, "Chase just tried to kill us. He's your traitor, and we need to leave now. The locals are on their way, and we are out of time."

Gerard looked ready to argue until he saw her bleeding. "Get back to the penthouse." He pulled off his jacket and wrapped it around her shoulders and said, "Go with Luke and Sean, they will see to your wound. I will take care of everything here."

Rhen moved over to Drake, tied to one of the chairs with what looked like rifle slings, and cut him free. The man's face was already swelling, and he was still seething with anger, but one look from Rhen kept him from saying anything stupid for a change. They ran up the stairs and piled into the vehicles. Elle was in the back of a black Mercedes with Sean. She winced when he pulled away her suit jacket to see the bullet wound.

"It's a through and through. You got lucky. The bullet missed bone and arteries. It's going to hurt like a bitch, but you'll heal. You need anything?"

"I could use a drink and a damn good explanation."

CHAPTER 15

Elle almost smiled when the men surrounded her walking through the hotel. She had anticipated them blocking anyone's view of her to avoid unnecessary attention, but this showed they believed she was a target. 7 must have called ahead because the manager was waiting at the door to let them in, and a second man was standing with him holding a black medical bag. The man didn't say anything and avoided looking anyone in the eye, but he was all business when examining her wound. *House doctor.* His demeanor made it clear this was not his first experience patching up a bullet wound here, and he disapproved. Fortunately, it seemed he took his practice seriously.

She sat stoically while the doctor did his work, watching the men around her. The reactions were varied, but each of them was uneasy. No one talked while the doctor worked, and that just increased the tension in the room. When Rhen and Drake entered, Drake looked at her with a scowl, but averted his eyes and didn't say a word. It was impressive the sway Rhen had over the idiot. Believing Elle had taken a bullet for his friend meant something, even to that douche bag. Given his views on women, it had to be messing with his head. *Damn.* She hoped he wasn't too preoccupied. She needed one more thing from him.

Once the doctor was finished, he gave her some medicine and instructions on wound care. Elle barely listened. She was an expert in that area. She kept her focus on the men. The second the door closed behind the doctor.

"What the hell is going on?" Max asked, breaking the silence.

Elle didn't answer, just looked at Rhen. He needed to be the one to tell the story. After handing Drake some ice, he did. Rhen didn't shy away from the details. As he talked, Drake's face turned almost purple with anger. She started a mental countdown in her head. She would push things if Drake didn't do what she wanted in five, four, three—

"It's awfully fucking convenient that Rhen was the one who just happened to be sent out in the crosshairs and that Gerard's boy was the shooter," Drake said right on schedule. "Where's that fucker now? The bastard set us up. That's why he left Chase behind. All the rest was just a bullshit smokescreen. He wanted us gone and came up with an excuse."

A moment of stunned silence met his rant before they all started denouncing the accusation with varying degrees of force. Words were lost in the confusion of everyone talking at once, but Drake had done what she needed. There was doubt now, each of them had it, and it would fester. As they thought about the events of the last couple of days and all the unusual behavior, that doubt would take hold deeper.

"But why would Gerard want Elle dead?" Sean asked.

"How the fuck should I know?" Drake growled. "She got in the way somehow. Or maybe she's a bad lay. Who cares."

"Or maybe Chase just went rogue. If he had managed to kill us, he could have sold any story he wanted to Gerard. Probably continue with whatever operation he had going with us as his patsies," Rhen said.

"That bitch wouldn't even take a piss without Gerard's approval. There's no way he'd turn on him. I'm telling you, we're being set up," Drake argued.

Luke spoke up for the first time. "For what? Why would he need to set any of us up?"

"Why don't we fucking ask him? Oh wait, he's not here. Convenient. Wonder why? Probably meeting with his boy to find out why he couldn't finish the job," Drake answered.

Keeping her face stoic, Elle said, "If he did set us up, then one of two things is going to happen now. He's either going to find a way to finish us or bury Chase. Since he likely didn't intend to take everyone out, my guess is that Chase is going to disappear for good."

"You guys are suggesting that one way or the other, we're vulnerable now. Whether from Chase, Gerard, or both. If you're right, then we're screwed. So, what do we do?" Sean asked.

They all looked at each other in silence.

That's when the door opened, and Number 7 entered, looking like he was ready for a fight. He walked straight to his bar and poured a very stiff drink and downed it. They watched him without comment, waiting for him to speak.

Placing his hands on the bar, he looked ready to explode. "Chase is in the wind. I went by his place, and it's been torched." He practically growled the words. The looks on everyone's faces confirmed exactly what Elle wanted. Chase had disappeared, just as she predicted. The question for each of them now was whether it was because he ran or because 7 took him out to cover his tracks.

Rhen mirrored the look on 7's face. "Your man just tried to kill me, Gerard. What the fuck was that? Did you order the hit? Was this all some kind of elaborate plot?"

Elle did not expect such a strong outburst from Rhen. Her money had been on Drake stirring the pot more. This was better.

"Watch yourself, Rhen. I'm not in the mood to deal with any more bullshit right now. If I wanted you dead, you'd be dead. And I would do it myself." Anger blazed in 7's eyes.

"Then explain how your second-in-command just royally fucked us all without your knowledge. Or do you really expect me to believe that it was just coincidence that you left him outside and then sent me right into his ambush?"

7 hurled the glass in his hand at the wall with such force that it shattered, shooting shards everywhere. He pulled the gun holstered at the small of his back and pointed it at Rhen's head. Every man, except Rhen, automatically drew their own weapons and aimed them at him.

Rhen stared at 7 defiantly, waiting for an answer.

The power in the room had shifted, and 7 felt it. Snarling, he countered with questions of his own, "How about you explain what you and Drake have been plotting for months now? Or did you think I hadn't noticed? Was this all part of your plan?"

"What's he talking about?" Max asked.

"He's just trying to cover his ass," Drake responded.

"They've all seen you two together, just like I have. They know. You've been planning on taking me out, haven't you, Rhen? Looking to step right into my business. Did you think that if you discredited me that you could take over? Slip into my position and magically fix everything? The CIA picks me up, and then, amazingly, the leaks stop, and shipments are clean again?"

The men were too seasoned to telegraph their reactions, but Elle saw jaws clench. *Thank you for sealing the deal.* Each man could easily see how Number 7's version of the story—where Rhen was the mole—was plausible, which muddied the waters even further.

Rhen didn't take the bait. "So, my master plan is to walk myself into the line of fire of your shooter and count on someone to save my ass? What then? Admit it, Gerard. You were either behind this to give you a reason to get rid of us, or you were so obsessed with this idea of us taking over your business that you missed the real threat."

"You really think I would sabotage my own business to keep you from taking over?"

"How do we even know any of it was real? You're the only one who's seen this so-called evidence. I heard you say that the only person to access your security system was you. And you were the one who 'found' the tracker. And then you take out Drake and send me to my death."

"But why send Elle to watch you then?" Luke asked.

"I'm betting it wasn't his idea to send anyone. She would've just been collateral damage."

Silence followed Rhen's response. They all knew the suggestion wasn't his. In their minds, if Elle had not followed him, Rhen would be dead, and none of this would have come to light.

The anger in 7's eyes was still there, but he started laughing maniacally. It sent chills through Elle.

He lowered his gun, grabbed the open bottle of rum, and drank directly from it. "I underestimated both your ambition and intelligence, Rhen." Looking around at the guns still pointed at him, he continued, "Clever to make counter-accusations, but you never denied that you were the leak." He took another drink before he added, "Regardless of whatever has happened here, we need to figure a way out because it affects us all."

"Like we're going to trust you," Drake said.

"What choice do you have?

"What does that mean?" Max asked.

7 leveled a glare at Max. "It means that for better or worse, the only way to dig ourselves out of this mess is together. It's going to take a lot of time and effort to repair the damage. If we clear out the trackers and shift locations, we can start rebuilding. If Chase was the leak, then they just lost their source."

"And if we want out?" Luke asked.

7 grimaced and gripped the bottle he was holding even harder. "Why would you want to do that? My business will survive this setback. We still have our merchandise and, once I show my contacts that the problem has been dealt with, we will continue making money."

Luke squared his shoulders and met 7's eyes. "And how are you going to show that the problem has been dealt with? Because no matter how this went down, I don't want to be forced into whatever is going on between you. I came to do a job and get paid for it, not to get involved in some bullshit power struggle."

"I'm not giving you another chance to put a fucking bullet in my back," Drake said.

"You wouldn't be worth the cost of the bullet," 7 said. "You have a valid concern, Luke. This business requires professionalism and loyalty. Anyone who wants to go can. I won't stop you. But, be warned, try to cross me or steal from me, and I will hunt you down."

The men continued to hold 7 in their sights.

"If we stay, what would happen next?" Max asked.

"We would secure the merchandise someplace else and then hunt down Chase. As long as he is out there, he's a loose end and a liability to all of us. Including whatever plans you had, Rhen."

"Fuck you, Gerard. We're out. Any of you who want to come with us are welcome. Leave this high and mighty prick to deal with his own shit," Rhen said.

"You'll never be able to recreate what I've done. Without the right introductions and contacts, you might as well be just another street thug selling scraps."

Rhen turned and walked out of the room.

Drake stood and followed him out but kept his weapon pointed at 7 the entire time. The door slammed behind them. The tension in the room remained, but no one else moved a muscle, indecision warring inside the remaining men.

"Unless any of you has more to add to whatever this is, maybe everyone could relax and put away the guns. We're supposed to be professionals, right?" Elle asked, exasperation coloring her tone. Looking at 7, she added, "Since you're already back there, I could really use a drink."

At that, the remaining guns lowered.

7 started making her a drink, suddenly oblivious to everyone else in the room.

Scanning the men's faces, she could see each was deep in thought, so she decided to push them. "You're not doing yourselves or anyone else any good just standing there. I suggest you either sit and have a drink or go and do whatever you need to do to get your head straight."

Sean, Luke, and Max looked at each other, hesitating.

Elle worried for a moment that they were going to sit. But, after looking at the dark expression on 7's face,

Sean and Luke left the room. Max lingered a little behind the other two but decided to follow them out.

Alone again, Elle waited for what was to come next.

Number 7 handed her the drink and sat down beside her. His expression was very dark, and she could tell he was planning his next move. She sat quietly, biding her time.

Finally, he asked, "Are you staying with me, belle?"

"After all this, I'm reconsidering my options. A lot depends on how you move forward."

"I suppose I can understand that. But I can assure you that I will be fully operational again soon."

"I assumed. A man like you would plan for things like this."

He smiled ruefully and took another drink. "I don't know if there is really any way to truly plan for something like this. But, yes, I do have plans in place to deal with business being compromised."

"So, what's the next move?" Elle asked.

"I already have people at the showroom moving my merchandise. If anyone tries to move on me now, they will find the site empty."

"Are you leaving DJ?"

"For now. My merchandise is being split between my yacht and a cargo ship. Once the more valuable cargo is loaded, my yacht will return for me."

"Can you trust your crew?"

"Not sure I can trust anyone at this point, but I have to risk it. The real question is, are you coming with me? Coming back from a breach like this will demand that I come back stronger than ever. A new angle, new associates. It's the perfect time to rebrand with a beautiful woman as my lead." He stroked Elle's cheek tenderly before his eyes traveled down to the bandage on her shoulder. "I had no idea what would happen tonight. I swear that I had nothing to do with what happened to you."

"I've had worse," she said. "How long before you have to go?"

"About an hour."

Climbing into 7's lap, Elle straddled him. His hands moved to her hips and pulled her body against his harder. She kissed him and pulled back just enough to whisper, "I'll come with you."

His mouth clamped down on hers, almost angrily.

She didn't resist and forced herself to return his level of passion. Pulling away from him after a few moments, she said, "I need to get my gear. Should I meet you here or at the boat?"

"I'll meet you at the boat. Don't worry about bringing much. I will make sure you have everything you need."

"See you soon."

Number 7 walked her to the door. Kissing her again, he said, "One hour, and we'll be free of all this and off on a new adventure." Elle nodded and smiled before walking away.

She could feel the unseen eyes on her as she made her way back to her hotel room. Alert to a possible ambush, she didn't feel as though she could really breathe again until she had a door between her and the rest of the hotel. She barely got it closed before her entire team was in front of her, all talking at once, asking if she was okay. Julian's face had a noticeable strain on it, and Eve looked sick with worry. "Nice shooting, Julian. Could not have been more perfect. And I'm fine. This is nothing."

"I swear I almost had a heart attack waiting for you to come back, Elle. I was so worried. Are you sure you're okay?" Eve asked.

"I don't have a lot of time. Jack, I need you to figure out how to get a fix on 7's yacht. I'm going to need a ride from it once we hit international waters, and the Agency will want to pick it up. It's going to need a new owner and crew soon. Tex, Julian, walk with me. I need you to brief me on how things went while I change and pack." She saw disapproving and concerned looks, but for the time being, it looked as though her team wasn't going to argue with her.

As Elle moved around her room, gathering items to include in her bag, Tex and Julian filled her in on how the mission went from their perspective.

"The khat worked like a charm. A couple of bags and damn near everyone at the port disappeared," Tex said.

"I was worried that the lack of activity might alert 7 or his team that something was wrong, but in the heat of the moment, no one noticed," Elle told them.

"The break-in was child's play for Jack. We got in and out without any issues. Julian set up where we planned and watched our backs the whole time. After we planted the trackers and locked everything up, I took Jack to the getaway vehicle, then circled back to wait for the lookout to be posted."

It had been a gamble, but Elle bet on 7's hubris and hadn't been disappointed. The man had counted on Chase's complete devotion, and they exploited it.

"Once the guy was alone, Julian became my eyes. Chase never knew I was there. I pulled his cell phone, wallet, and keys then weighed the body down and pushed it into the water. The sharks can take care of the rest. After that, it was Julian's show, and I pulled back to the rally point with Jack."

Julian picked things up from there. "There were a lot more shadows than we'd anticipated, so it was difficult to see you check your watch. That was easily the most challenging shot I've ever taken."

Elle could tell that Julian had been worried that he had done his part a little too well.

"Once you got to the truck Tex pre-staged, I took off down the far side of the building using the rappelling line. It worked perfectly. I was out of there and back to the rally point in no time."

"While we waited for Julian, Jack and I went through the wallet and confirmed the location of Chase-boy's residence. As soon as Julian made the rally point, we went for the house. With the keys and Jack's skills, we got in fast. We grabbed stuff from the closets and drawers and shoved them into a bag to make it look like Chase left in a hurry. Then we pulled the SIM card from the cell and smashed both on the office floor. On the way out, we set a fire in the office, including the ID and credit cards from the wallet," Tex said, finishing the story.

"Well done, guys. You gave Number 7 enough evidence to convince him that Chase had gone into hiding. The set up was perfect. Now, Chase will be seen as a threat they can't account for."

"Are you sure about this next part, Elle? And before you take my head off, remember that you are going to be alone in close quarters with a bunch of bad guys, and you've lost blood already. It's crazy. There has to be another way."

Elle could hear the concern in Tex's voice. Smiling, she said, "There probably is another way. And you're right, this is crazy. That's why it's going to work."

CHAPTER 16

Back on the deck of the sleek yacht, Elle tried to lose herself in the night, breathing in the salt air to calm her churning emotions. Her chosen course was the best option, but knowing that didn't ease the sick feeling in the pit of her stomach. The rushing water deafened all other sounds, but she knew she was being watched. A now familiar touch circled her waist, and his body pressed in against her back. For a long time, they just stood there in silence.

"I've given orders to put as much distance between us and DJ as quickly as possible. We'll keep running at full speed and won't make a port call for a couple of days."

Turning to face him, Elle said, "How much of a strain will that put on this toy of yours?"

"It's not ideal conditions, but she's more than capable. The ship will handle it better than the crew will. I've let them get soft."

Smiling seductively, Elle looked around to verify they were alone. Rubbing her body against his, she asked, "So what do we do now? Seems we have some time on our hands."

"I can think of a few welcome distractions." He dipped his lips to hers and kissed her softly. Elle deepened the kiss and intentionally stoked the fire between them. She knew what he liked, and she used that knowledge shamelessly. Pushing 7 so that his back was against the railing, Elle began undressing him. She worked her way down his body, lingering around his groin, teasing every nerve and driving him wild.

His groan of satisfaction made it clear he didn't notice the sting of the needle in his thigh as she took him into her mouth. She turned up the intensity to keep him distracted as the poison took hold. He was a dangerous man, and she couldn't chance a head-on confrontation. It had to be this way. She couldn't risk everything for her ego or guilt. His hand awkwardly bunched in her hair, and he tried to pull her up, the first indication that the end was close. Elle stood and moved to kiss him, but he stopped her. *Not good.* If he realized what was happening before it was too late, she was going to have her hands full.

"What is it?"

"Something's wrong."

Elle looked around, searching for a threat, using the ruse to put some distance between her and 7. "I don't see anything."

7 staggered and grabbed the rail to steady himself. Elle kept a look of concern on her face, but when he finally looked up at her, the accusation in his eyes was unmistakable. He knew.

She moved fast, striking at his throat to keep him from trying to call out. He dodged the strike, but in his weakened state, he couldn't avoid it entirely. The motion pushed him off balance, but he wasn't going down without a fight. He lurched at her, and she used his momentum to pull him sideways and sweep his leg. 7 went down hard.

He struggled to turn onto his back. 7 was pale, sweating, and having a lot of difficulty breathing. This was it for him. Nothing could save him now. Elle stood just outside of reach, watching. "It was you," he said.

She hesitated before answering, "I was tempted to really go with you."

"Why?"

"You were a number on a list."

7 almost looked like he was smiling when he stopped breathing. Elle stood looking at the body for a few minutes before moving. She told herself it was to make sure she wasn't being baited into approaching too soon, but felt tears as she knelt down. She swiped at her

205

eyes angrily before clearing everything out of 7's pockets. All she found was his cell phone and a key card. She used 7's hand to unlock the biometrics on the phone and then disabled all the security settings. Pocketing both items, she positioned herself for the next task— the body.

There is no easy way to move dead weight, particularly when the body is significantly larger than the bearer. Rolling 7 over onto his stomach, Elle placed herself at his head and hooked her arms under his armpits. Using every bit of strength, she raised the body until she could get a leg under the torso, below the center of gravity. She was sweating and breathing hard, the body felt like lifting a truck, but she couldn't give up. Elle ducked under the upper body after a short pause, placing the torso across her shoulders in a fireman's carry. She wiggled to even the weight as much as she could and heaved upward.

The body felt like it barely moved, but it was enough to get it over to the rail. Careful not to get entangled, Elle shifted the weight, and with one last heave, tipped the body overboard. Panting, she leaned against the railing and watched it fall into the water. Within seconds, it was out of sight. She stood against the railing and forced her breathing back to normal. Taking a few moments to straighten her hair and clothing, she did her best to make sure she didn't appear disheveled. Retrieving her bag, Elle pulled out a suppressed 1911 and mentally mapped out her next move.

The crew.

Turning toward the correct ladder well, she descended into the yacht's engine room. There were two men in the room; she shot them both in the back before they even knew she was there. Taking a few seconds to verify that no one else was in the room, Elle holstered her weapon in the small of her back and closed the door behind her as she exited. The weapon's suppressor made it cumbersome, but she needed to mask the sounds of the gunshots as much as possible. Walking through the passageways was when she was at her most vulnerable. There was little room to maneuver and no cover. If any of the crew became suspicious of her before completing this mission, she would be in for a fight. She needed to look like she belonged wherever she was, and not present a threat.

She moved methodically through the interior of the yacht, covering as much ground as possible. It was a race against time to take out the crew before anyone could raise the alarm. She found two more men in the galley. They looked surprised to see her and a little wary. Elle moved to the large refrigerator and pulled it open as if she owned the place. "You guys have any ice cream on board?"

They looked at each other before one answered, "Yes, ma'am. We have several flavors that we can bring to you. You don't have to trouble yourself."

"It's no trouble, I prefer to do things myself from time to time." She smiled at them before saying, "I could use some help finding it, though."

That got them moving. One went to the cabinets to pull out a bowl, and the other motioned for her to follow him. "Over here in the walk-in freezer, ma'am."

He moved to the back of the space and motioned to a shelf, "We have several different flavors, vanilla, chocolate, strawberry, mint choco—"

Her blade severed his windpipe before he could finish speaking. Only a liquid gurgling followed. He staggered, and she ripped his head backward to force him to fall away from the shelves. It tore the wound open further, driving the man's focus to his throat. Any thought of struggle disappeared as shock claimed him, which allowed her to cushion his fall to the ground. He wasn't dead yet, but she had no choice but to turn her back on him. Grabbing a container of ice cream, Elle walked out of the freezer calmly. "This will work if you can't find the cookies and cream," she called back over her shoulder.

The other man looked up from the counter as she walked over. Placing the container on the counter, she opened it and said, "It's been a long time since I've had mint chocolate chip, so it's not a big deal."

"The cookies and cream is on the top shelf, I saw a few containers…" He walked over to the open door and stopped when he saw the body on the floor. As soon as he was in line with the freezer, before he had time to register what he saw, the bullet struck. Elle shot him in the back of the head. His body pitched forward as he crumpled to the floor. Stepping over him, Elle put a bullet in the first man to make certain he was dead, then pulled the second man's body far enough into the freezer to be able to shut the door. She studied the area around the freezer, looking for any sign of foul play. Nothing.

Returning the gun to its hiding spot, she scooped some ice cream into the bowl and tossed the container in the trash. Grabbing a spoon, she left the kitchen, casually nibbling at the treat. She barely noticed the flavor. There were three more men to deal with, and two of them were fighters. While all of 7's crew have likely had some combat training, two of them had been hand-selected for security. Given the type of man 7 was, that really said something about the caliber of the threat she was currently hunting. They would be roving, which left too much to chance for her taste, but there wasn't another option. Trying to draw them out would take time, or tip them off that something was wrong.

Her instincts tugged at her conscious thought. *Topside.* She hoped that being out at sea had lulled them into a false sense of security. They would be watching for pirates until they were in international waters, making it more likely to miss an insider threat. Elle returned to the deck and sat in one of the chairs with her ice cream. Selecting a spot that gave her as much field of view as possible, she settled in. Every second that passed made her skin crawl. The bodies of the men she had already killed could be discovered at any moment. She'd be in for a full-on assault if that happened.

Keeping her demeanor casual, she kept eating the ice cream as though she didn't have a care in the world. After about ten minutes, she noticed a shadow moving on her left. Turning, she saw one of the security guards come around the corner.

When he saw her, he paused before he said, "Nice night."

"Yeah, too nice to be inside quite yet."

"Shouldn't you be with Gerard?"

Elle raised an eyebrow and met his eyes. "I think I'm old enough not to need someone to hold my hand."

The guard shifted slightly. "I didn't mean any offense. I just assumed he would want you with him."

"He wanted some time alone. After tonight, I wasn't about to press."

Elle turned back to her ice cream and the ocean view. After a brief hesitation, the guard continued on his rounds. The moment she was in his blind spot, she drew her weapon and fired—two to the back and two to the head. The first two shots struck body armor, but the next two put him down. She made a mental note about the body armor for the second guard. Moving to the downed man, she searched for a radio. She found a small push-to-talk handheld one and a key card. Pocketing both, she took the guard's Glock and prepped for her next move.

Even if she had disposed of the man, she wouldn't have been able to clean the blood and brain matter in time. She removed her suit jacket and draped it over her arm. Then, she poured the remains of the ice cream on the sleeve and tossed the bowl overboard. Tucking the Glock into her waistband at the small of her back, she held the suppressed 1911 under the jacket and got moving. Assuming the guards used overlapping routes, Elle continued in the same direction as the first man. Leaving the body where it was, she started a mental countdown, estimating how much time she had left to get this done. Two to three minutes, max.

The radio crackled in her pocket, and every muscle tensed. "Bow clear, moving aft." He was just around the corner and moving her way.

Elle walked with a determined stride and planted herself directly in the man's path.

His surprise made his hand automatically move to his holster.

"It's about damn time!" she shouted. "Everyone scattered the moment I needed something. What the hell am I supposed to do about this?" She waved at the stain on the jacket and raised her arm as though to give him a better view. The second his eyes focused on the stain, she extended her wrist, bringing the 1911 in line—two rapid shots between the eyes. The second guard crumpled at her feet.

Dropping the jacket, she removed the second guard's weapon and tossed it overboard. While she believed the captain was the only crew member left, she didn't want to leave herself open to attack. Moving back through the interior of the yacht, she listened for movement. Standing outside of the bridge, Elle used 7's keycard to open the door. She moved in fast. The captain reacted the moment he saw her but not the way she'd anticipated. He dove for cover.

What the hell?

A second later, he popped up and shot at her.

Taking cover, Elle's mind whirled. *How did he know? Did he send out a distress signal?* She needed answers, which meant she would need to take him alive for now.

Moving to her right, she quartered every angle to avoid presenting an easy target to her quarry before moving around the console. The captain hadn't seemed like a trained fighter, but now she wasn't certain. A bullet tore into the floor just behind her foot. Judging from that shot, he wasn't a marksman. He'd also given away his position. *Time to end this.*

Elle leaped up and vaulted over the console. Her shoulder screamed in protest, but speed was necessary. She closed in on the captain before he could react and shot him in the arm.

He cried out in pain but tried to get another shot off.

She kicked away the pistol and shot him in the other arm. He sprawled on the floor in front of her, snarling in agony.

"Who are you, really?"

The man lay there panting now, refusing to answer. Elle stepped on his right arm and applied pressure.

He screamed.

"Let's try this again. Who are you?"

His voice cracked when he finally spat, "I work for the CIA."

Her blood froze. *No fucking way.* "Bullshit."

"I was recruited over a year ago."

"Who's your handler?"

"Go to hell."

Elle applied more pressure to the wound. The man screamed again but still didn't answer. She put the barrel of her gun against his kneecap. "Talk or lose the knee."

"You're going to kill me, anyway, bitch. He warned me about you. They know you're dirty. They'll be coming for you."

She studied the old man for a while, and her mind raced with different possibilities. None were good. Marcel believed what he was saying. He wasn't lying. That meant one of two things: she had just busted up an off-the-books operation, or there was a rogue agent at the CIA. Unfortunately, since Marcel had been warned about her, that pointed to the rogue agent. To make things worse, the rogue element had to be someone who knew about her. That was an extremely small pool of people, and each would be detrimental to the mission.

Marcel was bleeding all over the place, and he was getting paler by the second. Elle took out her knife and watched him stiffen.

He put on a brave face, but she could tell he thought this was it. She cut away his sleeves and bound his hands together. He groaned again and again, but she didn't relent. He was dangerously close to succumbing to shock. She didn't want him to die, but he couldn't be allowed to move freely.

Next, she needed to stop the bleeding.

Getting to her feet, she walked to the rear of the bridge and ripped open a cabinet with a red cross on it. Inside, she removed the emergency medical kit. Returning to Marcel's side, she rummaged through the contents until she saw what she needed: Quik Clot gauze and pressure bandages. Rolling him on his side, she ignored his cries and looked for clear exit wounds on each arm and nothing on the chest. She had to make sure that the bullets didn't bounce off a bone and end up in the chest cavity. Seeing two clear exit wounds and nothing on his chest, she cut the gauze and started to pack the wounds. Marcel thrashed against her, screaming.

"If you want to live, stop fighting me," she said. If he heard her, he didn't show it. The Quik Clot gauze was causing a chemical burn in the wound, essentially cauterizing it from the inside. It was painful, but it beat bleeding to death. Elle kept going, doing what she could to save the man's life.

Then, suddenly, he went slack.

She stopped to check for a pulse. It was weak but there. He had lost consciousness. *Shit. Get moving!*

Working on a limp body was a hell of a lot better than one that was in fight mode. Elle finished dressing the wounds by using pressure bandages to secure the gauze and keep constant pressure. Once she was done, she pulled a blanket from the kit and covered Marcel. She then pushed the medical bag under his legs to elevate them. Checking his radial pulse confirmed that she hadn't cut off the circulation to his limbs. Satisfied he wasn't going to die on her in the next couple of minutes, she pulled her satellite phone and called her team.

"Ready for pick up already?" Tex asked.

"Change of plans. We have another player in the game, and I need intel. I'm holding onto the captain. He's been injured and needs medical assistance. Get the Embassy to give you their medic, and grab a couple of extra bodies for security. This is going to be our new base of operations for a while. Get a helo to bring you out to the ship. I'll need you for the interrogation, and Jack needs to figure out how to run this ship. It's state of the art, so I imagine everything is computerized. He should be able to operate it from his laptop. Get Eve to find anything she can about Captain Marcel."

"What happened, Elle?"

"No time to get into it right now. You need to move fast. Grab all our shit and clear out of there. Get ready to spend some time at sea."

"Anything else?"

"Yeah. Don't trust anyone."

CHAPTER 17

Elle watched Marcel, waiting for any indication he was regaining consciousness. She checked him regularly to make sure his pulse was steady and that the bleeding was under control. He'd survive. Now, she needed information. After an hour, his breathing changed, and she saw his face grimace. Grabbing her satellite phone, she took a calculated risk and called Director Calloway on his private line. If the man had wanted her out of the way, he could have done it at any time.

"It's about time you checked in, Ms. Anderson. Or have you forgotten your responsibilities as team lead when we lose an asset?"

"Apologies, sir. I wish this was a status update. It's been a fluid situation, and we have another significant issue. We have either a rogue agent or an imposter in play."

Silence.

Elle watched Marcel out of the corner of her eye. She was confident he was awake and listening.

"I assume that you have more than a hunch to back this up?"

"The captain of the target's ship, he claims to work for us. He was prepped to take me out on the word of his handler. The man must be in deep or just easily manipulated. One way or the other, his handler decided he was expendable to kill me. This is either personal, or they were afraid of exposure."

This theory was met with more silence.

Elle could feel Marcel's anxiety. She continued, "I've requested for my team to meet me onboard the target's vessel and bring in a security detail and medical from the Embassy."

"Medical?"

"Yes, sir. The captain was wounded while trying to kill me. He's stable now but needs medical attention. The security is for his benefit, but I don't know who to trust. If his handler thinks he'll give him up, he's a dead man. He's probably safest with me, but I need to keep on mission, not babysit. It's a gamble that no one at the Embassy is compromised by this son of a bitch, but it's one we have to take."

"What do you need?"

"Information. The captain would be the best place to start, but I don't have time to deal with him right now."

"I'll make sure the Station Chief knows this is a priority, and I'll be monitoring progress. There's a team not too far from you that will be redirected to assist." Calloway paused before adding, "I really hope you're wrong, Ms. Anderson."

"I wish I was. Whoever did this hates me enough to risk exposure and lose an asset. He's unstable, and we need to find out who they are before they do any more damage."

"What's your plan?"

"I'll offload the captain with the Embassy personnel, and then we'll move on to Italy."

"We need to assume that your mission has been compromised," Calloway said. "An operational pause to assess the level of compromise is your next step."

"I don't have time for that, sir. I need to keep the momentum if we have any hope of succeeding."

"It's protocol, Ms. Anderson, and it's there for a good reason."

"Which is exactly why I need to keep moving. This is all connected somehow. If it's a rogue agent, they'll be expecting an op pause. They'd use the time to get away or set up defenses. I need to keep the pressure on. It's the best chance we have to finish the mission and expose this guy."

Calloway sighed. "Keep me apprised of any new developments."

Disconnecting from the call, Elle checked her watch and turned to Marcel.

His eyes were still closed, but his breathing gave him away.

She watched him for a few minutes before she started her approach. "I know you're awake. I'm coming over to check your bandages. Don't fight me. In your condition, it would probably kill you to try."

He went rigid but didn't respond.

Elle moved to his side and remained alert for some misguided attempt at escape. His bleeding had slowed, but he had lost a lot of blood. "Your arms will need surgery, but you'll live. Medics are on the way. When they get here, you're not my problem anymore. Don't try to move until they tell you. You'll be weak from blood loss and could rip your wounds open."

Returning to the helm, she sat in his chair and watched the various monitors and gages. The yacht had external cameras forward and aft with infrared capability, which allowed her a near 360° view in the dark. An attack right now would be disastrous. The only chance she'd have would be if she had a head start. But she didn't like those odds.

The silence stretched out for a long time. Elle continued ignoring Marcel, letting his mind run wild while she studied her surroundings. When the time came to recheck his condition, she wasn't surprised to see him studying her.

"I'm coming over there again. Don't be stupid."

He remained silent but didn't tense up.

"If anything feels different, you need to tell me or risk losing it."

As she checked to make sure the bandages weren't cutting off circulation, he said, "Who are you?"

Elle gave a derisive laugh. "Thought you knew all about me? Or did you forget that you tried to kill me?"

"You were going to kill me."

"You sure about that? Let me guess, your handler told you I was here to kill you. Now, why would that be? Because of your connection to him? If so, you'd have more value to me alive.

"He knew all about you. He said my only chance to live was to kill you first."

"And you bought that?" Laughing coldly, she asked, "Are you so valuable that someone would risk taking on an entire team of highly trained mercenaries just to kill you?"

Marcel didn't respond.

"You don't seem like an idiot to me, Marcel, so I'm going to give the benefit of the doubt that you were duped because you don't know how this business works. Your so-called handler saw you as a liability when you told him about me. He pushed you into provoking me, which, in most cases, would have meant your death.

Since he viewed you as expendable, the coward sacrificed you to protect himself."

"No. You're trying to get into my head. I saw your gun. You were going to kill me."

"I'm not going to waste my breath. Think what you will. But if I were going to kill you, what was my end game? You've been watching me long enough to know I can't drive this thing. I had to change my plans and call for backup because you're injured. Not exactly something a dirty agent would do. Think about it." Elle walked away. "Would've made more sense to capture you to take me where I need to go. It would have been easy with the rest of the crew dead." She sat back in the captain's chair and resumed watching the monitors.

"What are you going to do to me?" Marcel asked.

"Keep you alive until I can pawn you off. You can be someone else's headache."

"What's that mean?"

"It means that you can waste another agent's time. As far as I'm concerned, you're nothing but a liability. If you've got nothing for me, I've got no reason to care what happens to you."

"So, you expect me to talk to get proper treatment?"

"I don't expect anything. You seem to have blind faith in the asshole who wanted you dead. You'll get proper treatment no matter what you say or do. But you better hope that your boy doesn't have any connections there. He's going to be pretty desperate to kill you now."

"I don't believe you."

"Don't care. It's simple. When an asset is picked up by our people, they're released when the handler IDs them. When you don't get released, because your handler is a fraud, start watching for assassins. You might want to start thinking about self-preservation."

"You're just trying to scare me," Marcel said, but he didn't sound convinced.

"If you're scared, good. Means you might still make it out of this. Life's about choices."

Elle returned her attention to the monitors, kicking her feet up onto the console.

"What are you doing?" he asked.

"Waiting."

"Seriously? You're just going to leave me here?"

"Until I can get rid of you, yeah. You've already put me behind schedule." The satellite phone rang. "Go, Tex."

"We're inbound. Need some lights so we can land this thing."

Elle turned back to Marcel. "Where are the lights for the helo pad?"

He didn't answer.

"Look, one way or the other, my team is coming on board. The longer it takes them, the longer it takes for you to get medical care."

Marcel finally said, "The panel on your right, open it. The helo pad lights are at the bottom on the left."

Elle found the correct switches and flipped them on. These next few minutes could get interesting if there were any pirates in the waters around them. Now that she was all lit up like the Fourth of July, she was completely exposed. Even with her team coming in, it would be ugly unless they were flying in a gunship. She secured the bridge door and went on heightened alert, watching for any sign that something was wrong.

Some of her tension eased when she recognized the sound of the approaching bird, but she stayed focused. The helo pad was above them, so she turned on a third, much smaller, monitor that showed the landing zone. She didn't breathe until she saw the bird land and the security team scan the perimeter. From their body language, they didn't see a threat.

She heard them barrel her way. Tex was in the lead, his frame obvious despite all the shadows.

"Sounds like you've had a hell of a night. So, what's next?" Tex asked.

"I've already softened Marcel up for you, but he needs to be broken. I recommend crafting your approach to place blame on his handler and throw in some incentives. Should be easy since he really was set up to die. I think he's starting to see that he was played, but he'll never admit it to me. At least not in the time we have. And time is something we can't spare. We need as much information about his handler as we can get before they take him back to DJ."

"That's going to be harder than you think. They were only planning on being on the deck for thirty minutes."

"Do what you can. I've been in his head for the last couple of hours. He's primed. He just needs you to tip him over the edge."

Tex nodded and walked over to where the medic was getting Marcel ready for transportation. Eve was standing next to Jack at the helm. "What do you think, Jack. Can you handle it?"

"This thing is awesome! It's fully automated and has a state-of-the-art operating system."

"Was that a yes?"

"Hell, yes! I can program the yacht to do exactly what we want, but I don't know the rules for being at sea. Isn't there some sort of code?"

"Don't worry, Captain Jack, I think we'll be able to figure it out," Elle said.

"I'll research navigation and port requirements. Are we still heading to Italy?" Eve asked.

"Yes. This thing will blend right in with all the cruise and private yacht traffic that flows through that area. The port we're going to is located to the northwest of Rome, so we'll need to figure out transportation to take us into the city."

"I can handle that." Elle turned at the sound of Julian's voice.

He looked like he was all business. "We just finished the sweep of the spaces. All clear. We found six bodies and tossed them overboard, but no sign of your target."

"He went overboard hours ago. Number 7 was the first to go."

Julian searched her face for what seemed like an eternity before he nodded and said, "The crew is prepping to return now. Anything else you need from them?"

"Stall them. We need to give Tex as long as possible with Marcel before they take off."

"I'll do what I can, but they have a tight timetable. We interrupted preps for another op to get them to bring us here."

"Understood. Eve, you and I will bring all our gear into the conference room. Once we're on the move, we'll regroup there."

They moved with a purpose. Eve followed Elle to learn her way around. Once they were done moving their gear, Eve set up with a laptop in the conference room, and Elle returned to the bridge. Marcel had been moved to await transport, and she could hear the rotors of the helicopter spinning up. She checked the monitor and saw the pilots finishing their pre-flight checks. Julian and Tex were both standing off to the side. Tex was still talking to Marcel, and she could see that the medic looked concerned. Was it because he was worried about his patient overexerting himself, or worried about what he'd say?

Elle watched the Embassy team and Marcel board the helo and take off.

Then Tex and Julian returned to the bridge.

"Jack, how are we looking?"

"We're good. I can leave it on autopilot while we're in open water, but we'll need someone here to watch for other vessels when we get into high traffic areas. There's a collision alarm and some automatic maneuver functions, but it's pretty basic. It's better to have eyes on. It looks like it's going to take us a few days to get to Rome if we stay at normal cruise speed and don't stop for anything."

"I'll take first watch," Julian said.

"Okay. But, first, I need you all in the conference room." Elle turned and walked out, Tex, Julian, and Jack following her.

Once they were all seated, Elle asked, "Did you get anything, Tex?"

"Just a first name for his handler and contact number. Hopefully, the genius twins can do something with it." He fished a piece of paper out of his pocket and handed it to Eve.

Eve read, *"Thomas. Original."* Then, she paused before adding, "This number is based in the U.S." She looked at Elle.

"Whoever this is, they know who I am and are determined to take me out. He's a threat to the mission and one hell of a curveball. We need to ID him and fast. Three days is a really long time to delay getting to Rome, but we need it. We need to do a deep dive into our operations and determine how much has been compromised. On top of that, we need to take a hard look at Hans Waite, Number 6, our next target. Something has felt off about his profile since we first ID'd him. We can't risk more surprises. I'm making the call to sacrifice some time to gain insight."

"What's the plan?" Tex asked.

"We set up shop here. This will be our new base of operations for the time being. Eve has the UN Convention on the Law of the Sea and maritime and port protocols. While we're each on watch, we can get our sea legs. Jack, run the phone number and push all the data to Eve. Give her whatever support she needs. Eve, while you're waiting for the new data, go back through every detail we have on Number 6. I don't doubt your research, but something doesn't add up. We need to figure out what. Look for anything that seems odd, no matter how small. Tex, you and Julian need to go through all our comms since we've been in DJ. See if anything could be connected to Marcel trying to take me out tonight. We need to know if it's someone internal to our operations or not."

"We're on it. What are you going to do?" Tex asked.

"It's been a rough day, and I need some rest. I'll be right across the hall if anything comes up."

"Get some sleep, Elle. We've got everything handled," Eve said

Tex smiled at her as he kicked his heels up on the table. "I don't know. From the suite at the Kempinski to this? I'm not sure I can handle these working conditions."

Elle knocked his feet off the table. "Get to work, cupcake." She grabbed the bags they'd brought her and walked down the hall to the first room on the right.

It wasn't until Elle was in there that it hit her: She was in Number 7's room. Her stomach turned, and a wave of sadness struck. Why? He was a task, that was all. *It wasn't real.* She felt tears again. Ignoring them, she used the shower and then forced herself to lie in his bed. His scent surrounded her. The tears didn't stop until she fell asleep.

CHAPTER 18

Elle slept fitfully and woke a few hours later covered in sweat. She was exhausted, but her mind wouldn't allow for any more sleep. Cleaning up, she dressed and went to check on her team's progress.

"I don't know what to make of this, Elle, but it's definitely odd," Eve said. "The number that Marcel gave us, it mirrors the activity of Hans Waite, I mean, target number 6. At least most of the time. They diverge enough that it's clear it's two different people. Thomas is someone close to Number 6."

"What the fuck did we just stumble onto? How the hell is this connected?" Tex asked.

"I don't know yet. But at least we know a little more than we did before. Eve, did you go over Number 6's details? Anything stick out?" Elle asked.

"That's the really weird part, Elle. Knowing what we know now, it makes even less sense. The man seems to be clean, outside of the account activity. I double-checked everything. I even found him on social media at a few charity events. The data doesn't add up."

The pieces clicked in place for Elle. "That's because he's a pawn. Eve, you're brilliant, and so is this guy, Thomas. Can you show me the charity coverage?"

"Sure. But I don't understand. Do you think he's being coerced?"

"No. I think he's oblivious. Someone close to him is using his access to make their own deals without 6's knowledge. It's the perfect set up. If anyone picks up the lead, one of two things happens: They wave it off because the facts don't add up. Or, they take out an innocent man, one that can never compromise the true target, since he doesn't know he's a fall guy."

"How do you know they aren't in it together?" Julian asked.

"I don't. But it fits. Why would one partner allow the other to be exposed while keeping such a low profile? The whole operation is compromised if 6 goes down. There's no benefit for Thomas."

"Just because they're playing on the big stage doesn't mean they aren't idiots," Tex offered.

"Thomas is definitely an idiot but not in the way you're thinking. If it weren't for his hatred of me, he could have walked away, and no one would have been the wiser. It was a brilliant plan. But he took a shot at me, instead, and wasted an asset in the process. He risked everything and exposed himself. That screams that it's personal," Elle said.

Eve pushed her laptop around for Elle to see. "Here are the two most recent posts about Number 6. He seems to like the charity circuit. Here is one from last month, and here—"

Elle snatched the laptop.

"What is it?" Eve asked.

"Eve, I need you to pull up any images you have with Number 6's entourage."

"Okay. Can I have the laptop, please?" Elle released the computer back to Eve and started pacing the conference room like a caged animal.

"What's going on, Elle?" Tex asked.

"I need to be sure. Give me a few."

He nodded.

The tension in the room rose with every second that passed. Each click of the mouse pad and every keystroke seemed amplified as Elle waited for Eve.

"Here you go. It's Number 6 arriving at the IMF charity fundraiser two months ago. It looks like he has a personal assistant and a couple of bodyguards." Eve stepped back to let Elle stand at the laptop.

Elle's blood ran cold.

"Thomas is Tom Matthews. And he was CIA."

"Was?" Julian asked.

"He was a superstar on the fast track until he crashed and burned. He got relegated to desk duty and

233

unraveled. He couldn't handle not being the star anymore," Elle said.

"What happened to him?" Jack asked.

"Me. I was the new girl, and I was making a name for myself. Tom was my first handler. But he chose to use the position to set me up for failure. For whatever reason, Tom saw me as a threat. He almost got me killed. Afterward, he tried to cover up what he had done, but his plans fell apart when I survived. Calloway relieved him of his position while they investigated what happened. Instead of waiting for the results, he resigned.

"How long ago was that?" Tex asked.

"Four years. Shortly after the dust settled, Director Calloway offered me this position. I'd put myself on his radar with the way I handled what he saw as a 'no-win' situation."

"What happened to Tom?" Eve asked.

"He disappeared. But the resignation would have allowed him to create an impressive resume for the private sector. It looks like he applied his skills to the fields of private security and crime. He's our link to Daesh, not Hans Waite."

"So, what's next? Tex asked.

"You, Julian, and I will take the brunt of the bridge watches to allow for Eve and Jack to build a target profile on Tom, our new Number 6. We also need to figure out the logistics of getting to him. It will take us about an hour to get into Rome from the port."

"You should probably sit this one out. If this guy even gets a glimpse of you, it's all over," Tex said.

"Wait a minute. Are we talking about killing him? He may be a traitor, but he's still an American. Shouldn't we just have him detained? Or arrested? Or something like that?" Eve asked.

"Why would his nationality make any difference? He's a number on the list and a link to the Daesh power base that has to be severed. Would you be asking if he were any other nationality?" Elle countered.

"But you know him. And he was CIA, once. Doesn't that make a difference?" Eve continued.

"It makes him more dangerous. And now that he's tried to kill me twice, knowing him doesn't faze me at all," Elle said.

Eve pursed her lips but didn't push.

"If you can't handle this, Eve, speak up. We can make arrangements to get you home."

It was clear Eve wasn't comfortable with this course of events but shook her head. "I don't want to leave you guys. If you're going, so am I."

"What about the rest of you? If you want out of this part, now's the time," Elle said.

There was a long pause before Tex broke the silence, "I don't like it, but I get it. This guy isn't just a traitor, he's financing terrorists. Too many have lost their lives fighting these guys for me to have much sympathy for anyone helping them. You going to call Calloway?"

"Yes. He needs to know. But, first, I need to hear from Jack and Julian."

"I guess I'm staying.'

"That wasn't very convincing, Jack."

"I know. But it's the best I can do. The only thing I'm certain about in this whole thing is that you will need my help. So, I'm staying."

"I'm staying too. You are playing in dangerous territory, and it's become personal for all of you. You'll need perspective to keep from going too far," Julian said.

"There is no such thing as too far now. We're going to finish what we started, one way or the other."

Julian's face was unreadable, which bothered Elle. "You volunteered for first watch. Go ahead and get to it," she said.

Though Elle was dismissing him, Julian's expression didn't change. His eyes never left hers, though. Without saying a word, he inclined his head and left.

"Elle, let's take a walk so the kids can get started, and we can talk," Tex said.

His expression told her more than any words could have. Tex was worried. *Fuck.* "Not now, Mike. I have to call Calloway." She grabbed the satellite phone and walked to the main deck.

Calloway picked up on the second ring. "What do you have?"

"It's Tom Matthews, sir. He's the rogue element, and our actual link to Daesh."

"Do you have proof?"

"Yes, sir. We were able to get a number and a name from the captain before he was taken back to the Embassy. The number matched our original target's movements enough to determine that he was someone close to him. When we pulled footage of some events they attended, I was able to positively ID Tom. It's him. There's no question."

Calloway cursed.

Elle couldn't remember ever hearing the man curse before. She waited in silence as he mulled over the news.

"He has to know that you're coming for him. And it's personal for both of you. This is no longer your mission, Ms. Anderson."

"No, sir. This is still my mission, and I'm the best person to see it through."

"You're too close to this. I can have personnel in place within the hour to pick him up."

"And what happens when they fail? If he gets away, then both my life and my mission are in jeopardy. Again. Tom might have lost it, but he knows exactly how the Agency operates, and he was once considered your best. He'll see a tactical team coming a mile away. He won't see me. I can't wait around for him to have another chance to kill me. I need to end this up."

"Are you planning on disobeying me if I direct you to stand down?"

Elle clamped her jaw shut so hard it hurt.

"If I can't trust you anymore, Ms. Anderson, then you're not much different than Tom. And I have no place for you."

Elle felt sick as a wave of conflicting emotions crashed through her. She was teetering on the edge, and she could feel it. All she wanted was blood, but was it worth losing everything else? Was she breaking like Tom did? "No, sir. You'd be making a mistake. But I would follow your direction. I'm hoping that you won't give that order."

Calloway said, "Captain Marcel is dead. It happened before anyone could talk to him and was made to look like a suicide. That tells me Tom is well connected and has compromised others within our ranks. We will be following procedure in DJ with investigating this as a suicide, which I have no doubt will get back to Tom. That should convince him that his identity is safe, and he'll continue business as usual."

"But now you need to be concerned that Tom has other assets in place within our lifelines that would alert him to an assault."

"I'm speculating, but it doesn't seem likely he would risk having Marcel killed if he knew he'd been identified.

That level of risk is more in line with a last-ditch effort to avoid exposure. It's the most plausible explanation given the circumstances."

"So, what does that mean for me?" Elle asked.

"It means you get your way. For now. But let me be clear: I have serious reservations about both this course of action and with your state of mind. Tom has put us in a very vulnerable and precarious position, and I don't mean just from the mission's point of view. He's a risk to all our operations and agents. So, I'm willing to risk allowing you to continue with your unconventional approach. Do not make me regret it."

"You won't, sir."

"We'll see. One way or the other, we'll be having a very long conversation when you return." With that, Calloway hung up.

Elle winced at the thought of what that would likely entail.

She sat down in one of the deck chairs and watched the water pass by for a while. She knew he was there but tried to ignore him. Eventually, she asked, "What is it, Tex?"

"What did Calloway say?"

"I'm sure you can figure it out since you were eavesdropping for at least half of it."

"All of it, actually. But it was a one-sided conversation from my perspective." He walked over and lounged in the seat next to her.

Elle found herself chuckling, despite her irritation. "We're cleared to move on our new Number 6. Calloway understands that it's the best chance we have to nail him."

"Elle, I know you aren't going to want to hear this, but it has to be said. You need to sit this one out. And don't go crazy on me. If you weren't so close to this or so damn stubborn, you'd see it too."

"Why is everyone trying to sideline me?"

"Probably because you would never do it on your own, and you're going to get yourself killed in the process. The target knows you, Elle, and has a serious hard-on for taking you out. You can't let it get personal. Especially not now."

"What's that supposed to mean?"

"Come on, Elle. You know better than anyone that you've been off, and you've sure as hell taken a beating these last few days. You need to rest and take a step back. We're supposed to be in this for the end game, not to get distracted by bullshit."

"This son of a bitch has tried to kill me twice!"

"So? He's probably not the first and, knowing you, he won't be the last. Are you going to make it all personal? Didn't you tell us they were just names on a list? Tasks to get done? What makes him special?"

"I can take him out and be done with this."

"So can I. You shouldn't take the lead on this one."

"This guy is good, Tex. I'm not kidding. He was a rising star for a reason. And you're right, I know him. That's why it has got to be me. I can anticipate him."

"Fine. Then I'm going with you."

"No, stay here with the team. They'll be vulnerable," Elle said.

"Julian will be here. I'm coming whether you want me to or not. If you try to leave without me, I'll follow you. Then you'll have to contend with me, while not exposing yourself to the target. Probably best to just include me before I accidentally ruin your grand plan."

Elle didn't have a response, so she just glared at him.

He smiled widely. "Good. Now that we have that settled. What's the plan?"

"Sometimes, I hate you."

"I know. Stop stalling."

Elle went to the bar and poured two drinks. She handed one to Tex and said, "We're going to need to go OTB."

"Over the beach? Are you talking old school or using the speed boat?"

"Old school. We're swimming in."

"Shit. Well, at least it's the Mediterranean."

"Number 6 will be monitoring all major ports of entry. The yacht will draw attention, but when Eve and Jack debark and get taken around by Julian, anyone observing will assume they're rich tourists with their bodyguard. They won't fit any description that would

241

warrant a report to 6, and he wouldn't recognize them anyway. The only risk we have is if the boat is ID'd. We'll have to change the yacht's registration info before we pull into port."

"I vote for renaming it *Titanic*." Tex grinned. "What? Too soon?"

"Your jokes are getting worse by the day."

"I'm comedy gold, you just don't understand brilliance."

Elle shook her head in mock exasperation before she turned serious. "This is going to be ugly, Mike."

"I know. That's why I'm going with you." His tone belied his casual posture.

They sat there, thinking, sipping their drinks.

"Don't keep pushing Julian away," he said, breaking the silence. "Whatever's going on between you two, we're going to need him. As far as I can tell, he hasn't done anything wrong. He deserves better," Tex said.

Elle wanted to tell him to go to hell but refrained. He was right. Julian wasn't to blame for her guilt or her shortcomings. Yet, she was punishing him.

"One problem at a time, Tex."

"Well, we've got a couple of days before we get after it. I suggest you take some time to heal, get your head straight, and then make peace. He's a professional, he can take whatever you throw at him."

"We've got shit to do."

"And it'll get done, Elle. Stop being a stubborn ass. You know it's the only course of action that makes any sense right now. We'll update you whenever you want, so go get some rest. You can't do much today, and you're beat all to hell. Julian and I will take care of the watches for now and tag you in tomorrow. You can make your plans while you're on watch."

"Dick."

"Love you too."

CHAPTER 19

Elle's mind was almost as bruised as her body, but she did what she could to promote healing and rest. It wasn't easy. Her anxiety grew with every passing hour, and she was angry with herself because of it and felt cowardly, too, which made things worse. It wasn't until an hour before her watch that she forced herself to go and talk to Julian.

She found him doing a roving patrol on the main deck.

When he saw her, he inclined his head and kept walking.

"Julian, stop. Please."

He turned.

She still couldn't read him. "I owe you a lot, but for now, I'm hoping you'll let me start by apologizing. There's no excuse for my behavior, so I won't try to justify it. All I can say is, I'm sorry."

"Apology accepted."

When she didn't say anything further, he turned to leave.

"Wait. That's it?"

"Do you want there to be more?"

"I figured I would get some response. A lecture, questions, something."

"I could definitely accommodate any of those options if you'd like. But I don't think you really want to go down that road right now. You've got things you need to deal with, Elle. You didn't make me any promises. I can handle the rejection and still do my job."

"I didn't reject you."

"Didn't you?"

Elle clamped her mouth shut. She should have just let Julian leave. This was definitely a conversation she did not want to have. Elle's stomach turned, and she struggled to keep eye contact.

Julian stepped closer as he waited a moment for a response. When she didn't say anything, he nodded once, then walked away.

Shit. Her chest tightened with regret. But he was right—this was not the time. Elle let out a shaky breath and mentally shook herself.

She went to the conference room and found Eve and Jack. "What have you got for me, guys?"

"Not much, I'm afraid. Our new Number 6 is a ghost. Other than the information we could find from his time with the Agency, the only thing we've been able to dig up is that he's listed as a security expert and international affairs advisor with the same bank that…um, our old Number 6 works for," Eve said.

"You can call him Hans Waite, Eve. He's not a target anymore. I'm sure of it. And I'm not surprised that 6 has covered his tracks. I'd be disappointed if he didn't."

"Since we kept hitting a dead end with 6, we shifted focus to Hans. He may not be the bad guy, but he seems to have him in tow a lot." Eve turned to Jack, and he picked up from there.

"I was able to find an RSVP to a charity event this weekend. It's at the Rome Cavalieri. We're assuming that since Hans is going, 6 will be there too," Jack said.

"Good assumption. What's the event?" Elle asked.

"It's a masquerade. Apparently, they're holding it in the hotel's private park, and it'll be catered by one of their restaurants. What is a Michelin star anyway?

"It means you won't find grilled cheese on the menu. What time does the event start?" Elle asked.

"Eight, and scheduled to last until two," Eve said.

Elle smiled. "Perfect. That's our way in. Jack, do you think you can get Tex and me on the guest list?"

"Yeah. What names do you want to use?

"We're going to need something new. We have to assume that Marcel passed our names on to 6. Pick whatever you like, but don't go too crazy. We'll have to modify our IDs to match."

"Gotcha. Two wicked cool secret identities coming up."

"I'm heading to the bridge for watch. Give me everything you can on the port, the route in, the hotel grounds, and the charity holding the event," Elle said.

"No problem. We've got most of that already. Give us a few more minutes, and we'll get you everything," Eve said.

• • •

The next forty-eight hours passed quickly and quietly. Elle focused on what was coming. This was going to be a nut roll. When she walked into the conference room, the entire team was there and ready to go. Like her, Tex had his wetsuit hanging open around his hips to avoid overheating. Their gear was laid out on the table: two rucksacks that had been rigged with foam to float with near neutral buoyancy in the saltwater. Inside, they had everything they would need, from weapons to clothes, in dry bags. It was approaching sunset, and she planned to hit the water as soon as they had the cover of darkness.

"Go, Eve," Elle said.

Eve used the screen on the far wall of the conference room and started with an overview of the area. "The best place for you and Tex to hit the beach is about one mile north of the port. It's going to be rocky, but it shouldn't be anything you can't handle. And it will help lower the possibility of having someone there. Even after dark, there's a high probability of people being on the beaches on nights like this."

Tex nodded. "We're good with that. Keep going, Eve."

"Once you're onshore, there's a train station about half a mile away. That'll be the best place to acquire a vehicle."

"Why, Eve, I'm shocked that you would even suggest that we would ever do something like steal a car," Tex said.

Eve sighed and continued, "It should take you about an hour to get to the hotel from there. Parking will be valet, so you may want to avoid that unless you can find a car with keys. The Rome Cavalieri is a stunning hotel and, while their park isn't large, it's perfect for a function like this. There will be security, both Carabinieri and private. There are several entrances to the grounds, but they are gated and will be monitored."

The screen showed an overview of the hotel grounds. It then moved to display the logo of the charity the event was sponsoring: *Doctors Without Borders*.

"No wonder 6 wanted to tag along. Their members have placement and access that's worth a fortune. Given the right leverage, he could easily turn any number of highly connected individuals. They would all have plausible reasons to be coming and going from hot spots all over the world that he could exploit," Elle said.

"Do you think he's looking for future assets or handling ones he already has in place?" Tex asked.

"I would say both. The ones he already has would feed him information he could use to bump and develop new contacts. Do you have anything else, Eve?"

"Just the hotel schematics and the weather. Do you need anything else from us?"

"You and Jack will head out with Julian after we pull into port. Dress to match the yacht. Julian will be your personal security. Jack, Julian, do what you can to lock this place down. We don't want anyone gaining access while we're gone. Go and enjoy Rome but stay alert. If anyone's watching the port, they should lose interest quickly, but we need to keep up appearances. Stay out for a couple of hours or until we call you back. If any of you feel like something's off, don't second guess it; head straight back here or to the Embassy. Do not underestimate what this guy is capable of."

"What are your contingency plans?" Julian asked.

Elle looked at Tex. "Tex and I are on our own for this one. If we go down, there is no backup."

"This is Italy, not Iraq. It doesn't have to be that way," Julian said.

"It does. But you're right, it's not Iraq. It's worse. We're about to try and take out a rogue American spy, on foreign soil, without host nation knowledge or consent. This is a black op with absolutely no legal status. If we fail…well, let's just say it's not going to go well for us."

"Before you even ask, I'm still in," Tex said.

Elle nodded. "Okay, if there's nothing else, let's get moving. Sun is setting, so it's about time to get this show on the road. Tex, I'll meet you in the bay in fifteen minutes."

As her team filed by, Elle waited. She grabbed Julian's arm as he started past, prompting him to stop. She waited until they were alone before speaking. "I know things aren't right between us, but I'm counting on you. If the mission goes south tonight, it will be up to you to take care of Eve and Jack…and maybe Tex."

"Don't worry about Eve and Jack. I've got them. But what do you mean about Tex? He's going to be with you."

"He may be coming with me but, if things get too intense, I'm going to finish it alone. Which means Tex may need an extraction. He won't leave by choice. But, if things go the way I think they will, he won't have much of one."

Julian gave her a hard look. "If you know it's going to go bad, then you need to adjust tactics. Don't let your emotions get the better of you."

"I'm not going to debate this with you. And I don't have time to try and ease your concerns. I know what

I'm getting into better than any of you. Right now, all I need is your word that you'll do as I ask. Please."

He searched her face, but Elle didn't know what he was hoping to find. Eventually, he nodded once and walked away. At the door, he said, "I'll do my part. Just make sure you come back, Elle. Don't get drawn into something you can't get out of."

Too late. "Thank you, Julian."

For a moment, it looked like he was going to say something else, but then he was gone.

Shaking off a pang of regret, Elle grabbed her gear and left to meet Tex in the bay of the yacht.

"You ready for this?" she asked.

"You kidding? A lovely evening swim in the Mediterranean? Does it get any better?

She bowed and gestured for Tex to take the lead. "After you then, princess."

"About damn time you recognized greatness." Tex eased into the water and pulled in his pack behind him. He shifted to the side to allow room for Elle. They both scanned their surroundings. Once they were satisfied, they started the swim to shore.

The water was cool but not cold. With the wetsuit, it was a pleasant swim. They took care to stay low in the water and avoid breaking the surface with their kicks. It was slow going pushing the packs, but it was necessary. They needed the gear, but the motion and noise would give them away if they moved any faster. The water was black and shimmered with reflected light from the night sky. Elle tried not to think about what might be under them. Predators came out in the night.

They both started treading water as they neared the shoreline. Tex held up his fist. Elle saw what had caught his attention. Two people were walking along the rocky outcrop they were heading for, looking for something along the waterline. When they sat down on the rocks, it was clear they weren't going anywhere.

Elle motioned to Tex, and they moved to a point further north.

Once they had enough distance to camouflage their presence, they moved onto the shore. The rocks were sharp, and the angles were challenging, but they managed to move through it. They found some concealment in a small grouping of trees and pulled off the wetsuits. They both wore workout clothing and pulled on tennis shoes from their rucksacks.

"We're going to need to pick up the pace to make our timetable," Tex said.

"I've been waiting for you to start moving at my speed. It's like running an op with my grandmother," Elle replied.

"Asshole."

Tex took off at a fast jog. Elle followed right behind, tightening the shoulder straps on her pack to keep it in place as much as possible to avoid creating hot spots.

It didn't take long to make the train station. It was fairly well lit, and the parking lot was over half full. Elle slowed down and started walking through the closest row of parked cars, placing her hand on the hoods of the vehicles she passed. It took about five minutes, but she found what she was looking for: a warm hood. The probability of this car owner returning soon was lower than the others. "This one."

"Does it have to be a Fiat?" Tex whined.

"It's Italy. At least they're easy to steal," Elle replied.

She broke the small pane of glass between the windshield and the passenger window. It was a design feature for the car that increased visibility for the occupants. The window was also great for thieves—it was just big enough to get your arm into the vehicle to unlock it but small enough that there was minimal glass lost and hard to spot at a glance. As soon as the door was open, Elle moved to the driver's side of the vehicle and pried open the steering column. From there, she studied the ignition system and bypassed the lock with a screwdriver. Then, it was just a matter of making the right connections to start the car.

Elle placed a towel over the broken steering column and put the car in drive. "Let's go."

"Why do you get to drive?" Tex asked.

"Are you kidding? You can barely fit in this car, let alone be expected to drive it. Just sit back and try to enjoy the ride."

"I suppose being chauffeured around Rome isn't so bad. As a matter of fact, I could get used to this," Tex said.

Elle chuckled but kept her focus on the road. Driving in Italy could be intense. Everyone drove fast and did not hesitate to take any space available on the road, even if it was a fraction of an inch away from someone else. It wasn't so much defensive driving as it was offensive. She needed to disappear into the traffic. Being pulled over was unlikely unless she did something really wrong, but she didn't want to tempt fate in a stolen vehicle.

The drive went smoothly. Before she knew it, they were in the city. She navigated through the streets following traffic flows until she found a small boutique hotel with available parking a few blocks from their target location. "Time to test our new IDs," Elle said.

"David and Nicole Webb. Wonder where Jack got these names from?"

"David Webb was Jason Bourne's real name," Elle answered.

"Nerd."

They went into the hotel. Their luck held, being a boutique location off the beaten path made it possible to get in without a reservation. No reservations meant they stayed off the radar longer. Handing over their passports, they waited to clear the standard security check. When the passports cleared without issue, they paid for a room upfront in cash, explaining their credit cards were not working, but they would be calling their bank as soon as they were able. Tex got the key and requested to have a taxi ready for them in forty-five minutes.

Once inside, Elle hit the shower first, as it would take her longer to get ready.

Tex organized their gear while he waited, and then they switched. They didn't talk, just moved with speed and purpose. They dressed and armed themselves accordingly. Formal wear made carrying weapons exceptionally difficult, but they had several special items from the yacht's stockpile that would be a huge help. Elle sheathed ceramic blades in her garter belt and added a small 3D printed gun. The firing pin and bullet were the only parts that were metal, and they were hidden as part of an intricate ballpoint pen. She holstered the derringer style pistol under the skirt of her gown, and placed the pen in her handbag. Tex was more likely to be patted down, so he carried a cell phone that had been modified to act as a stun gun.

Glancing in the mirror, they made sure they looked the part and that nothing was amiss. They made a striking couple; Tex in a tuxedo and Elle in a shimmery, black dress with gloves to cover the cuts on her knuckles. Putting their workout gear in the bags, Tex tossed them in the trash. They had no intention of coming back.

"I really liked those shoes. This fucker is going down hard for making me sacrifice them to come get his ass," Tex said.

"Let's just hope that's the worst we have to deal with tonight. You ready to do this?"

"I'm always ready. Are you?"

Elle knew what he meant, but she didn't answer. "I'm serious, Mike. We need to be ready for this to go bad in a hurry. Since we won't have comms, we need to have individual exit strategies. Make sure your contingency plan is to escape and evade on your own because I will be doing the same. We're a team, but taking this guy out is priority. If either of us has a shot, we need to take it and trust the other to care of themselves. The same applies if things go sideways. Don't try to be a hero. I need your word."

"I'll have my E&E plans ready, but you better not be setting me up so you can do some stupid shit all on your own." When she didn't respond, he added, "I'm trusting you here, Elle. You need to trust me, too. I know this one is personal, but we still have a lot left to do. Don't forget that."

"Fine. Let's get it done.

CHAPTER 20

The hotel was magnificent, and so was the clientele. As their taxi pulled up to the venue, Elle saw elegantly dressed guests walking through the security checkpoints onto the hotel grounds. Despite the grandeur of the location, she focused on the security posture and the gathered crowd, watching for her target. 6 was here, somewhere, and she had to see him first, or this op would fail. Pulling up to the curve, she waited until Tex came around the vehicle and helped her out of the taxi. She held his arm, and they sauntered up to the entrance.

The security personnel asked to search her bag and walk through a metal detector. Elle breezed through the check as though she didn't have a care in the world. Tex was asked to remove his jacket and turn out his pockets before going through the metal detector. He showed them his cell phone, wallet and chatted with them amicably. Collecting their things, they strolled toward the reception area.

The woman checking names asked for their identification, and Tex handed her their passports. Smiling, they waited while she ran their names through her tablet. It didn't take long for her to find them. *Well done, Jack.* She provided them with wristbands, their choice in masks, and then showed them a beautiful layout of the event. As the hostess pointed out all the amenities, Elle smiled and nodded at all the right places—though she was mentally marking the exits, security positions, and layout. She made mental notes of the key locations, too, that would draw the most guests, and where she could expect to find gaps in security coverage—the bathrooms.

Tex thanked the hostess as they put on their masks and moved toward the event. The bar leading out to the attached park was filled with people flowing in and out through large, glass doors. Elle's pulse raced when she saw Hans Waite holding court just outside in the main flow of traffic. He wasn't wearing a mask, and neither was anyone in his entourage. This event was about business for Hans, not socializing, and he wanted to be seen.

She scanned the crowd and found Number 6 standing off to the side, talking with a beautiful woman. Elle's grip on Tex's arm tightened, and she steered them away from the group toward the main bar. He let her take the lead without question. While he maintained a casual air and charming smile, Elle had no doubt he'd seen their target.

Tex ordered martinis and maneuvered to place his body between Elle and 6. Once the bartender walked away, he said, "He's well positioned there. You need to stay out of sight."

Elle watched 6 from their vantage point and fought the desire to walk up behind him and slit his throat. As satisfying as that would be, they'd never escape from such a brazen move. "We need to get him away from the group and into one of the holes in the security coverage. I've spotted three cameras so far. Our best play is the bathrooms."

"Guess that means I'm up. You can't exactly go strolling into the men's room without drawing a few curious stares."

"We don't know that he'll go anywhere without his meal ticket. We need to get him to the bathroom without Hans. Otherwise, that would put at least two men in there with you."

"Shouldn't be a problem. I'll still have the element of surprise on my side."

"Don't count on it," Elle said.

"What do you mean?"

"He'll be on alert walking into an area like that. Just like I would be. And he isn't above anything. He'll use Hans or any other person nearby to his advantage."

261

"So, we need to make sure the area is clear before we make our move. That isn't going to be easy with this amount of people," Tex said.

Elle glanced over at the bathrooms closest to where her target was standing. The entrance was partially obscured by a decorative wall. It didn't provide much in the way of concealment, but it would have to do. "Here's how we're going to do this. You're going to go and strike up a conversation with someone on the outskirts of that little group. Don't even acknowledge the target or his charge. Look for a chance to bump someone in the inner circle and make them spill their drink on 6. Even if 6 wants to stay in place, Hans will likely insist that the amount of security means he's safe on his own, and push 6 to go get cleaned up. You stay visible out there, apologizing to whoever was bumped, and offer to replace drinks. 6 needs to feel as though he was just collateral damage. Then he'll move to the closest bathroom to expedite his return. And I'll be waiting for him."

"Then what? You can't just kill him here. I might be going out on a limb, but someone will probably notice a dead guy. Kinda ruins the ambiance."

"I'm going to show myself, and get him to follow me out of here."

"Why the hell would he do that?"

"Extreme hatred and a god complex. Getting him away from everyone means he can't try to grab someone for leverage. Once he sees me, I'll move away from the crowd, so he'll have no option but to follow or risk losing me. He won't chance having me out of sight."

"And if he runs?"

"We follow. He goes down no matter what," Elle said.

"Okay. Ready to do this?"

"Yes. But first, I need you to promise me that you'll be on guard with this guy. Be ready for anything at all times. If you ever think you have the upper hand, he's got you."

"I promise. I know he's a serious threat. He won't catch me unaware."

Elle grabbed Tex's hand, palm to palm, wrapping their fingers in a silent acknowledgment of solidarity. Then, she nodded and walked toward the bathrooms to wait for her moment. It felt wrong letting Tex put himself in direct proximity to 6, and her skin crawled. But she needed him to be able to extract her target from the crowd without causing a scene. In this case, Tex was a means to the end.

She found a vantage point that allowed her to observe Tex near the bathrooms that was out of the target's line of sight. Several people were waiting for their significant others to return from using the facilities, so she passed the time by striking up conversations as though she were also waiting. She was speaking to a doctor from Nigeria when she saw the game start.

Tex had been having an animated conversation with several people. They were all laughing at what had obviously been a series of jokes when he made a large gesture that bumped a woman. She stumbled right into 6, who caught her, but not before she dropped her drink, which splattered on his shoes and pant legs.

Heads turned to take in the scene, and waitstaff converged on the group to begin cleaning the mess. Tex was using all his charm on the woman he bumped, with several polite apologies directed at 6, and offers to make amends by grabbing drinks.

Tex was convincing, and Elle was impressed. Perhaps too convincing. She could see him offering to buy 6 a drink at the bar to make amends, and 6 seemed to be considering. Then Tex brought his attention back to his shoes and pant legs, which is when Hans stepped in. She could see the discussion that she was sure would happen. Hans telling 6 he was perfectly fine. Tex gestured to the bar. Then, he took the arm of the woman he bumped and another woman's arm and walked over. *Perfect.*

6 moved her way. Elle pulled back into the alcove that separated the bathrooms and went into the ladies' room. She stood just inside the door and listened for 6 to pass. The temptation to follow 6 into the men's room and kill him was so strong she could taste it. But Tex was right. She couldn't just leave the body there. She heard the muffled sound of movement past the door

and the sound of another door closing. Elle left the ladies' room and placed herself at the entrance to the area and waited. It wasn't long before the door opened, and she found herself face-to-face with her past.

6 stepped out of the restroom and froze. Recognition was instant, but he wasn't surprised. *He was expecting me.* Elle had a fraction of a second to recognize the look that passed over his face before his hand went inside his jacket, and he pulled out a gun.

She threw herself out of the entryway just as the first shot tore through the wall behind her. The room exploded in chaos.

Elle ran for a series of booths. They wouldn't stand up to gunshots, but it was her best option to get out of the direct line of fire. Bullets followed her movements. Tables toppled over. Glasses shattered. People fell and were thrown to the ground. The screaming pierced her eardrums.

6 had no regard for anything or anyone. He fired indiscriminately, trying to kill her. Elle kicked off her heels, palmed one of the blades, and waited for him to reload. As soon as there was a break in the gunfire, she threw one of the heels in the only direction she could to draw his eye. It took down a row of glassware with a crash, and she was on her feet.

Elle went on the attack and ran at her target, throwing the knife at 6 as soon as she gained momentum. He had been ready for her. He finished his reload as he tracked her, but he hadn't factored in the knife. The blade lodged in his arm. The movement from trying to shield himself from the knife forced his aim to jerk away, and the bullet shattered a window just as Elle hit him. They went crashing to the ground in a tangle and began fighting for the gun. The blood running down 6's arm made everything slick, and she was hindered by the dress, but she fought like her life depended on it. Because it did.

"I should have killed you years ago, bitch."

Elle didn't acknowledge him. She focused on the fight. One wrong move and she'd be dead. It had only been a matter of seconds since he'd opened fire on her, but it seemed like a lifetime ago. She managed to get a firm grip on the hand with the gun, dropped the magazine, and then wrenched the weapon backward. 6's finger caught on the trigger guard, and she heard a satisfying crack before he screamed. The pressure on the trigger caused the round in the chamber to fire into the floor, sending shards of marble flying.

Now that the gun was empty, Elle went for another blade.

A booming voice shouted in Italian, "Stop! By order of the Carabinieri!"

They were suddenly surrounded by the Italian police with weapons drawn.

Elle was trapped in their sights, and there was no way out. She raised her hands and moved away from 6 carefully. She had no doubt he would not hesitate to kill her if he could—even now.

As soon as she was standing out of 6's reach, she was seized by the police. They put on handcuffs and then searched her. The remaining blades and the holstered derringer created a stir. 6 got on his feet. He was wounded but looked pleased.

Shit.

"This woman is an American assassin named Elle Anderson. I reported the threat against my employer when we arrived, and your supervisor let me keep my weapon. If he hadn't, she would have succeeded. She bypassed your security, but I caught her. She went for my gun, and I had to defend myself."

Son of a bitch.

Elle's mind raced. There wasn't much she could say to counter what they had witnessed first-hand. She allowed an incredulous look to cross her face. "This mad man came out of nowhere and just started shooting! Look what he did." Elle glanced around the room and caught sight of Tex. He was still shielding the two women he'd been with at the bar. They were clinging to him, but his eyes were locked on her. He was waiting for her to give him the next move.

She looked toward the door. *Get out of here, Tex.* When she glanced back, the pained look on his face showed he understood.

Elle returned her attention to Number 6. He was pleading his case with the Carabinieri, and they seemed to be buying it. However, he was still being taken into custody, pending further investigation. He wasn't pleased, but he was treating it like an inconvenience. Her stomach lurched. He must have someone inside the Carabinieri to assist him. Which meant she was in a lot more danger. An inside man could make sure any evidence against 6 would disappear or be attributed to her. He may even be able to have her killed. She needed to get out of this.

Elle started to wobble and grimaced. "I don't feel well." When a police officer grabbed her arm, she allowed her knees to buckle.

The officer barely caught her.

She gasped and cried out, drawing attention to her wounded shoulder. While the wound was several days old, the fight had re-opened it. Combined with the blood from 6, it was impossible to tell how badly injured she really was without a medical examination. She heard them call for an ambulance and maintained the ruse of fighting to maintain consciousness.

6 insisted they keep security on her, pushing a little too hard. Italian ambulances were small, and the Carabinieri were not pleased with having their jobs dictated to them. His attitude, combined with her performance, was shifting sympathy to her.

Keep going, asshole.

When the paramedics arrived, they placed her on a stretcher. They released her hands long enough to cuff her to the railing. One hand remained free.

She allowed her head to loll to the side. She caught the furious look on 6's face as they wheeled her away. Elle tried to spot Tex again but couldn't find him. Hopefully, he was honoring their agreement and was on his way back to the boat.

There was only room for one of the medics inside the ambulance. The other returned to the driver's seat. Elle removed a bobby pin from her hair and palmed it when the medic turned away. While he went about checking her wounded shoulder, she removed the plastic tip of the bobby pin. Using a junction in the stretcher, she bent the end ninety degrees. She cooperated with the medic to keep the illusion going, waiting for him to let his guard down. The second his back was turned, she made her move.

Inserting the makeshift pick into the handcuff lock, she "felt" for the release. It only took a few seconds. She unlocked the cuffs but didn't remove them. Elle remained on the stretcher until the medic returned to administer an IV, then she struck. She grabbed the man and placed him in a chokehold. He struggled fiercely, beating at her exposed wound. Elle held on, despite the pain. Once the man fell unconscious, she released him.

Elle took the medic's shoes, socks, pants, and jacket before cuffing him. Pulling off the bloody dress, she used some of the ambulance supplies to clean up her face and hands before dressing in the medic's clothes. She found a medkit and took it. The chances of the ambulance stopping were slim, so she braced herself at the door and waited for the vehicle to slow for a turn. When it did, she used the manual release to open the door. She paused for a second to assess where she was, then jumped.

She hit the pavement hard, the shock sending jolts of pain through her body. She allowed herself to tumble and barely managed to stop before hitting the curb along the road. It hurt, bad, and her breath was knocked out by the force of the impact. But at least she didn't break anything.

Elle was on a main road, and people were out on the street. The buzzing of voices made it clear her dramatic exit had been noticed. She was about to be surrounded. Getting to her feet, she tried to keep vehicles between her and the onlookers to make it difficult for them to give a clear description. Her body protested but responded.

As soon as her breath returned, she started to run, adrenaline dulling her pain. She turned off the road at the first opportunity. Elle kept making random turns until she felt confident that she could not be found easily. Once she was out of sight, Elle started looking for a vehicle. She had plenty of options but needed one parked someplace with enough screening to get in and out clean.

Turning on a side road, she found what she was looking for. She had just busted the window of another Fiat when she heard sirens approaching. Digging through the contents of the medkit, she found a pair of scissors that she used to pry open the steering column and made short work of hotwiring the ignition. Pulling onto the road, she drove casually, making her way north. There was a ballcap on the passenger seat, and she threw it on with her hair tucked in as much as she could. It wouldn't stand up to scrutiny, but she might escape immediate notice since they were looking for a woman with long hair traveling on foot.

She had a small window of opportunity to avoid getting caught in a police cordon. Her only advantage was that she had a slight lead. Elle drove main roads and stayed with the flow of traffic. The expressway entrance was just ahead of her when she saw flashing lights in her rearview mirror. *Fuck*. She needed to make the expressway before they shut it off, but she couldn't risk pushing her speed and standing out.

Her grip tightened on the steering wheel, and her pulse raced. She forced herself to maintain speed while she watched her pursuers close the distance. Gauging their rate of approach, she calculated her odds. They were slim at best. But she didn't have any alternatives. If she didn't make this, she would be forced to escape by speed or force. Both options were almost certain failures. If she got caught, no one was coming for her this time. Life in an Italian jail would be the best-case scenario.

A quarter of a mile and closing, she watched the line of cars behind her start to yield to the coming police vehicles. How far could she push before they wondered why she didn't yield? The last vehicle behind her slowed and moved to the side. She had about fifty feet left. She chanced it and pressed forward, slowing and drifting slightly to the side, giving the impression she intended to pull over. The police vehicles stopped at the intersection leading to the entrance to the expressway...directly behind her.

Her breath came out in a rush, and she felt faint for a moment. She hadn't realized how tense she had been, so she tried to shake it off and regain her composure. There would be intermittent patrols on the expressway, and they would be on alert. If the car she'd stolen was reported before she made it out, she was screwed. As the seconds ticked on, Elle had to fight to keep her anxiety at bay. *You can make it.*

Flashing lights warned her to stay away from the train station, where they had stolen the first car. The theft had been discovered, and the police were there taking the report. Driving past the location, she moved to the next road with parked cars. She mirrored the way all the other vehicles were parked and walked away.

Assessing her surroundings, she took off at a jog when all was clear. Running in socks was never pleasant, but at least they provided a small measure of protection for her skin. She needed to hurry, but one sharp rock or piece of glass was going to seriously impact her escape efforts.

Elle was exhausted by the time she reached where they'd hidden the wetsuits. The constant adrenaline of the last few hours was taking a toll. She almost cried with relief when she saw that Tex's suit was not there. He'd stuck to his promise. Now, she just hoped the team would still be there on her return. Tex would be watching for her, but a single swimmer would need to be within a few feet to be seen in the darkness.

Dressing in a rush, she started the swim and hoped the wetsuit limited the amount of blood in the water. Elle was halfway there when the yacht's engines fired up. Pushing as hard as she could, she used the last of her strength to close the distance. She lunged and grabbed the swim platform as the yacht started to move. The force of the current generated by the engines pulled her under just before two sets of hands snared her and pulled her on board.

CHAPTER 21

I t's over, Ms. Anderson. You're burned."

Elle couldn't believe what she just heard. "That can't be."

"Did you really expect to be able to just walk away from what happened in Rome?" Elle could hear the frustration in Director Calloway's voice. That told her more than words, and those were terrible on their own.

"How bad is it?"

"Your true name and picture are everywhere. Tom is using very lucrative connections to ensure that his version of events is being pushed in the media. Video of the incident showing you attacking him, images of your arrest, and interviews with the medic you attacked are breaking news on every major platform. It doesn't get much worse."

"So, what does that mean for us?"

"You're going to lay low, for now, use that yacht to bring you back to D.C. Once you're close enough, I'll be sending a helo to rendezvous with you and bring you all in for a full debrief. This is not open for debate. This is a direct order."

"My mission isn't done, sir."

"Yes, it is, Ms. Anderson. After your debrief, we will determine what happens next. But your time in the field is over. You and your team will be reassigned."

Tears burned her eyes, and anger tore through her. "There must be something you can do, sir. We can still finish this."

"No. You can't. Given all you've accomplished and the circumstances, I will look into options to allow you to stay with the Agency in some capacity. It will take time and a significant amount of influence to bury this story. But we will try to help you fade out of the spotlight."

She started to argue, but a hand on her shoulder suggested otherwise. She turned.

Tex shook his head and said, "Don't burn the few bridges you have right now."

The tears started streaming, and she swiped at them angrily. She choked on a sob, but managed to say, "We'll be in contact when we're just outside territorial waters, sir."

Calloway hung up without further comment. The click of the line disconnecting might as well have been a door slamming in her face.

She collapsed in the chair behind her on the deck.

"You want a drink?" Tex asked.

Elle didn't respond. She felt numb.

He went to the bar and returned with drinks and placed one next to her anyway. Sitting beside her, he said, "We'll get through this, Elle. Don't give up. We just need to let this part play out and figure out our next move from there."

"I'm burned, Mike. It's over."

"Horseshit. Burned or not, it's not over. The job isn't finished. We'll find a way."

For the first time in her life, Elle couldn't muster even a shred of the determination he was showing. She forced a weak smile. "I appreciate your confidence, but we need to be realistic."

"Just drink and relax. We have a few days of laying low while we make the transit home, and there are definitely worse places to do it than on a multimillion-dollar yacht. Let's use it to recharge and prep for whatever's next."

Elle felt...nothing. Like everything had been taken from her. Downing the drink, she sat, staring at the horizon. Her body and mind were broken, and now her purpose was gone.

• • •

The next several days bled together. Elle spent most of the time sleeping. She barely ate or spoke to anyone. At first, her team left her alone to rest and recover. But, after the first couple of days, she could see their worry. They all tried to get her to engage, but she refused. She just wanted to be alone.

When the helo finally arrived, Elle was the first to board.

They were taken directly to an offsite location and separated for debriefing. For twelve hours, Elle answered every question they asked. From the tone of the questions, she had fallen from favor and would be lucky to avoid an inquiry over what had happened with Red Shirt. By the time they allowed her to sleep, she was drained beyond belief.

As she was dressing in preparation for what she assumed would be another marathon interrogation, there was a knock at the door. She was surprised to see Wise walk in.

"Come with me, Elle. Please. Calloway wants to see you."

Elle followed without hesitation. They went to an office with a large bay window that looked out into a wooded area. In any other circumstances, she would have marveled at the view. As it was, she couldn't focus on anything other than Calloway sitting behind his desk. *This is it.*

"Please, sit down." He indicated the chair across the desk from him.

She took it obediently.

Wise stood off to the side, watching her.

"I've read the transcripts from your debrief so far, and they've confirmed many things for me. You are no longer fit for fieldwork," Calloway said, "That being said, Dr. Wise has lobbied on your behalf to keep you in the directorate in a support role. He volunteered to assist you through the transition. You've been of great service to our nation, and your sacrifices have been taken into consideration. For the time being, you will be placed on administrative leave, pending a full review. During that time, you will stay at your residence outside the city and avoid the press. We will need you to keep a very low profile while we work through this."

Elle felt like she was in a terrible dream world, but all she could do was nod.

Calloway studied her intently. "You will need to undergo a medical and psychological evaluation in the coming weeks as part of the review. We will schedule a time to bring you in when the heat has died down." He walked around the desk and stood next to her, forcing her to look up at him. "In the meantime, take care of yourself. You've pushed yourself beyond normal limits so many times, it was bound to catch up with you. Pending the results of the review, this may be your last chance to get back on track. I won't lie to you. If you can't do it, then you're no good to us anymore."

"What about my team?"

"They're also on administrative leave, pending the official review. Once that is complete, they will be reassigned based on the results."

"They were following my orders."

"Which will be noted accordingly. I can appreciate your concern for them. As of now, they are no longer your team. I can assure you, they will be taken care of."

Elle nodded. "What happens now?"

"There are follow-up questions that need to be answered. After they are finished, you will be given a chance to gather your things, and a car will meet you out front to take you to your house. We will be in contact. Please take my direction seriously, Ms. Anderson. It's in your best interest."

"Yes, sir."

Wise followed her out. "Elle, I have to ask. Are you thinking about ending your life?"

"It's already over."

"This part is, but it's not the end unless you let it be," Wise said.

"I'll never get back in."

The man in charge of Elle's questioning started to walk toward her, but Wise motioned for him to wait. "You asked me once why I picked you. Without purpose, I thought you'd be dead within six months. I was able to convince Calloway that you were the right candidate to send back into the field because of that. Your death seemed inevitable."

"Great to know."

"The one thing I never thought you'd do is give up. You may not be in the field, but this isn't finished. In fact, it's more challenging than ever. Something that should make you push harder. You quit, and you're not the person I thought you were, or the person your team believed in. You're the person Tom made you. And he's still out there." Wise nodded to her interviewer as he fished a business card out of his pocket. "When you're ready to get back into the fight, call me."

Elle looked at the card. It had a hand-written number on the back. Placing it in her pocket, she walked away.

Several hours later, she was in a black sedan heading toward her residence near Strasburg, Virginia. The evening scenery passed in a blur. Everything seemed dull and muffled. She fought tears intermittently throughout the ride, as her head just kept spinning. It was impossible to focus on anything other than the hollow feeling that kept trying to swallow her.

The car arrived at her house in what seemed like moments, as she had been unaware of time passing. Elle got out of the vehicle and made her way up to her house. It was night now, but her walkway used solar lighting, making it easy to see. She entered her security code into the keyless entry and walked inside. Elle flipped on the lights and started to walk through her foyer into the main part of the house.

Something is wrong.

Her instincts shrieked warnings, forcing the fog in her brain to clear. Someone had been inside her house. Moving to one side of the entryway, she continued toward the living room listening intently. Silence greeted her, but it felt off. Her skin crawled, and her heart started racing. There was a threat somewhere close. She peered into the living room and, at first, didn't understand what she was seeing. In the center of the room was an old, wooden chair with chipped paint and tattered ropes hanging from it like cobwebs. She didn't need to check to know the ropes would be stained with blood. Her blood.

She had almost died in that chair. Brutally beaten by a mad man half a world away—it all happened in that chair.

But here it was.

There was no doubt it was the one. *How?* The room started to close in, but she forced herself to move forward. A white envelope with her name written across it was on the seat of the chair. Elle knew this was a trap but couldn't stop. She felt eyes on her, but the need for answers overcame her sense of self-preservation.

She grabbed the envelope and tore into it. Inside, there was a flowery greeting card that read: *Missing You.*

Opening it, Elle read: *Agency protocols are so predictable, and you must be feeling a little worn out by now. Why don't you have a seat? Can't wait to catch up. See you soon.*

Elle dropped the card—t*hey're here*—and moved to a more defensible position behind her couch, just as all the lights went out.

CHAPTER 22

She could feel them somewhere in the darkness. Elle had one advantage: this was her house, and she knew the layout better than anyone. Until she could figure out where the threat would come from, and how, she had to assume they were prepared for a nighttime assault, which meant night vision goggles.

She heard a creak from the floorboards in her kitchen, then nothing. The air felt heavy as the silence stretched out, her vision was adjusting from being plunged into the darkness. She could just make out the outline of the damn greeting card lying near the chair she saw time and again in her nightmares. Elle had no doubt that Tom Matthews had written the note. But how did he get that chair? Tom and Mahmud Hussein—Number 3 on her target list, and the man responsible for her capture and torture—how were they connected?

A cold sweat crept over her skin. Both men had tried to kill her. Now it looked like they were working together to finish the job.

Movement caught her eye and ripped her thoughts back to the present. Two dark shadows moved into the living room from the kitchen. The assailants had a general idea of where she was, but not her exact position. That meant there was a spotter outside, which meant there was a sniper, too.

Shit.

Elle was not armed, but she didn't have a choice. *Time to fight.*

She had one chance at surviving this, and she took it. She leaped over the couch and lunged at her assailants.

Elle could just make out the form of the lead guy's handgun. She latched onto it and, instead of pulling, she pushed. Putting her full body weight into the motion, she trapped her assassin's forearms against her chest and drove forward with her legs. This forced the gun to lay flat between them. She didn't try to wrestle it away but slipped her index finger inside the trigger guard on top of his and applied pressure.

The gunshot was deafening after all the silence.

The second man stumbled and went down to one knee. The round impacted somewhere low in his abdomen. The shock of the attack gave her a chance to drive her elbow into the first assailant's throat. He gasped, and his grip loosened enough on the gun for her to shoot off a second round. It hit the second assailant in the head. This time, he crumpled.

The first assailant lunged forward. Elle's breath came out in a rush as he crushed her. They grappled for control of the gun. She was not positioned well enough to win this battle, so she did the next best thing—she used up all the ammunition. From the size of it, she guessed it had a fifteen-round magazine.

Using both hands to apply pressure, she forced him to fire off rounds. It took all her focus to keep the gun pointing away from her while fighting for control and counting the rounds. Bullets flew wildly in all directions. Thirteen, fourteen, fifteen, *click*.

Releasing her grip on the gun, she grabbed her assailant's head and drove her thumbs into his eyes. He shrieked and thrashed, clawing at her hands and pushing her away. She used the opportunity to lunge for the other man's gun. She got it as her assailant stumbled after her blindly. He was a second too late.

Elle rolled and fired, and he collapsed across her legs.

Yanking herself free, she crouched over the bodies. Her eyes had adjusted to the darkness, but it didn't help much. Everything was just different shades of black and gray. She had to rely on touch. Ears tuned for even the slightest change in sound, she ran her hands all over them. Elle didn't find anything on the second assailant besides more magazines for his pistol, which she took. Moving to the first man, she grabbed his extra ammunition as well. She was about to give up when she found a wallet.

Amateur.

She wasn't surprised. They hadn't handled themselves like a professional hit team—a fact that she was grateful for since they had caught her unprepared.

Though these two were dead, and she heard nothing: something was still wrong. She could feel it. *Why go through all the theatrics just to send two low-level thugs?* Tom would know she had a better-than-average chance of taking them out, even with the element of surprise on their side. So, what was his play?

It was a trap. It had to be.

Elle ran through the options. How would they set up an ambush? She had a car in the garage, but they had to be ready for that. She had a sneaking suspicion of how this was going to play out. One way or the other, she needed to move. Staying low, she crept to the kitchen.

She moved to the far side of the island and ran her hand along the wide baseboard until she found her biometric lock. Pressing her finger to it, she heard a small *click*. Opening the hidden compartment, she pulled out a small backpack. Her "go bag" had IDs, cash, a change of clothes, a lock pick set, a knife, and a first aid kit. Behind that was a case with her backup weapon and two extra magazines.

It wasn't much, but it was enough.

She added the recently acquired ammo and wallet to her go bag and slung both over her shoulder. Then, pulling open a drawer, she found the spare car keys, garage door opener, and a flashlight. Snatching a pack of batteries, she put fresh ones in the door opener and flashlight. Grabbing her cell phone from her jacket pocket, she pulled the battery out and tucked it away. Elle knew there was no way she'd be able to get a call out, as they'd be ready for that. The phone was a liability. It was now or never. She cracked open the door to her garage. Nothing. She opened the door further to give her plan the best chance of success, then backed away.

Staying below the window line, Elle moved to the furthest part of her house from the garage, collecting cushions from the sofa along the way. It was a guest bathroom with a beautiful metal bathtub. And right now, it was her saving grace. It had been mostly for show since she rarely had guests that stayed for more than a few hours.

Elle placed the cushions in the tub and then unlocked the window. If the pressure didn't shatter it, it would only take her a second to throw it open and leap through. Better than dealing with jagged shards of glass.

Pulling some cotton balls from under the sink, she stuffed them into her ears and climbed into the tub.

Ready to dive under the cushions, Elle held the garage door opener in one hand and the car keys in the other. *Here's hoping they used a shape charge.*

She pressed the opener and then the remote car starter a second later. As soon as she hit the button, she dove under the cushions and braced for it.

The explosion rocked the house.

Elle felt the pressure wave roll over her. Her head felt like it was in a vice, and she heard glass shattering everywhere. Pushing herself up as fast as she could almost made her blackout, but she shook it off and kept moving.

The window was shattered, but partially intact. She cradled the bags and held a cushion like a shield as she dove through it. She felt glass grab at her legs. She tucked and rolled awkwardly with her bags and refused to let the pain register. Elle pushed to her feet upon landing and ran as fast as she could make her legs go.

The first bullet whizzed past her a fraction of a second before she made it to the trees that framed her yard. The North Fork Shenandoah River wasn't far, and she had to reach it to have any chance of escaping. Moving through the woods after dark without night vision assistance was hazardous at best and pretty much guaranteed injury. But Elle didn't have a choice. She had no doubt they would have NVGs and be heavily armed. The only advantage she had was a head start, and all of the trees would make getting a clear shot almost impossible.

Unless they were right on top of her.

Trying to distinguish form in the darkness, Elle stumbled repeatedly but kept moving. Her body ached, and the strain on her eyes was not helping the massive headache she had from the percussion of the explosion. *Keep fucking moving.*

Her malaise from being burned and tossed out of the CIA was gone. She wasn't going down without one hell of a fight. She was so focused on her movement that she almost missed the changes in her surroundings. Two sounds registered simultaneously: boots thrashing through brush and the rolling river.

Time for a decision.

The river was shallow, so there wasn't much of a chance to hide in the water. Crossing it would slow her down significantly. She would be an easy target. But, if she could get across, they'd have no choice but to pursue her, exposing them, as well. Holding the flashlight in her hand, she threw caution to the wind and ran for it. She splashed into water that was just over her knees and kept going. Pushing harder, Elle felt like her lungs and legs were screaming.

Bullets sprayed around her a few feet from the other bank. Flipping on the flashlight, she pointed it behind her and kept running. The flashlight was one of those bright deals, a last-minute grab at the register found in every home improvement store. Right now, it was worth its weight in gold. The blast of light would be excruciating through NVGs. *You can't hit a target you can't see.* Their vision would be destroyed for at least a minute. This was her only chance. Setting the flashlight on the shore pointed in the direction from which she'd come, she ran and took cover behind a huge oak tree.

About thirty meters away, she spotted three men in tactical gear. *Only three?* The distance wasn't ideal for shooting a pistol, but she didn't have a choice. Bracing against the tree to steady herself, she did her best to control her breathing. She fired systematically, two rounds at each target, trying to make every shot count. Elle saw several of her bullets hit their targets, but the men didn't go down. *Fucking body armor.* She needed to shoot them in the head, and the odds were not in her favor.

They were firing wildly in her direction now. They couldn't see beyond the light, but they were firing in the last direction they saw her go. Pulling back to avoid catching a stray bullet, Elle caught movement out of the corner of her eye. She turned and fired almost automatically, two to the body, two to the head. That ingrained reaction saved her life. A fourth man was less than twenty feet away. He had flanked her position and would have taken her out if he hadn't been forced to maintain cover behind the trees to avoid being shot by his own guys.

With five rounds left in her magazine, Elle turned her attention back to the other men. They were pressing forward across the river, and one of them had managed to shoot out the light. Moonlight was all she had now, and her night vision had been affected by the flashlight too. Kneeling to give herself a sturdier base, Elle leaned out just enough to get her barrel clear of the tree and sight in on her targets. They were a lot closer, walking in a line and using suppressive fire, but they still couldn't see shit. It was now or never. She fired a single round at where each man's head should be based on the muzzle flashes. Two went down but the third kept coming.

The man bull-rushed the riverbank, screaming and firing rapidly everywhere. *Definitely an amateur.* Elle pulled back behind the tree and waited. By the time he made it to the shore, his gun was empty. She heard the gun go dry and leaned around the tree to put the last two rounds in his head. The silence that followed was almost painful.

She had to get out of there, but she needed information. Not wanting to be exposed, Elle went to the body of the man who had flanked her. She pulled off the NVGs and went through his pockets. Nothing. *Damnit.* Time was up, and she needed to go. Putting on the NVGs, she reloaded on the move. There was no telling what else Tom Matthews had in store for her.

Just the thought of his name made her blood boil. Elle had never hated anyone as much as she hated the ex-spy. Tom exposed her on the international stage, labeled as an assassin, and this was the fourth time he had tried to kill her. He knew all the agency protocols but pursing her back to the states showed a level of depravity that was mind-blowing. Burning Elle hadn't been enough. Tom partnered with a terrorist to play mind games before sending in a team to finish the job.

Elle stopped when it hit her: Tom and Number 3 were partners. Not just in this, but in 3's efforts to seize control of Daesh. Tom was the mastermind behind the plan.

Elle's capture and torture was part of an internal coup, and until now, she had assumed Number 3 had been the driving force. But she was wrong. Tom had pushed 3 to take over Daesh, to place him in a position of power that could be exploited later. Having her fall into their trap was just icing on the cake for him. Tom had been planning to take her out for a lot longer than the last few days, and acquiring the chair was proof of that. Sadistic son of a bitch. Burning her had been his best chance to leave her broken, exposed, and vulnerable.

Happy to disappoint, motherfucker.

Moving again, Elle picked up speed as much as she could. She needed to find a vehicle and get to D.C.

Because Tom wasn't going to stop until she was dead.

ELLE ANDERSON WILL RETURN FOR THE EXPLOSIVE SERIES FINALE:

SHADOW WAR

ACKNOWLEDGMENTS

It's impossible to truly appreciate the challenges of writing a series until you get to the second book. Just when you think you've got things figured out, reality punches you in the face. Luckily, I have people in my corner to keep me moving forward. Once again, thanks to Jake for sharing this wild ride with me, and for wrangling the kids to allow me time to write....and sometimes sleep. To Raina—your candor and support is priceless. Thank you for believing in me. To Arlen, Casandra, and Katie—thank you so much for all the support, motivation, and laughs. You guys are the best, and it's a privilege to have you in my life. And finally, to Ken Atchity and Lisa Cerasoli—again, thank you for pushing me to do better.

TO MY READERS

Thank you for reading *The Deeper Shadow*. Book reviews are often overlooked, but they are critical to helping authors gain visibility. Your feedback is important to me. Please take a moment to write an honest review on the e-retailer of your choice. Every review makes a difference. Have a great day.

—A. M. Adair

THE DEEPER SHADOW

Made in the USA
Middletown, DE
08 March 2022

62262365R00176